SWALLOWS PLAYING CHICKEN

SWALLOWS PLAYING CHICKEN

DAVID MENEAR

Mansfield Press

Copyright © David Menear, 2019
All Rights Reserved
Printed in Canada

Library and Archives Canada Cataloguing in Publication

Title: Swallows playing chicken / David Menear.
Names: Menear, David, author.
Description: Short stories.
Identifiers: Canadiana 20190190418 | ISBN 9781771262286 (softcover)
Classification: LCC PS8626.E543 S93 2019 | DDC C813/.6—dc23

Editor for the Press: Julie Booker
Design: Denis De Klerck
Cover Image: Pixabay
Author Photo: Peter Hart

The publication of *Swallows Playing Chicken* has been generously supported by the Canada Council for the Arts and the Ontario Arts Council.

Mansfield Press Inc.
25 Mansfield Avenue, Toronto, Ontario, Canada M6J 2A9
Publisher: Denis De Klerck
www.mansfieldpress.net

For Mom, and my kid sister Wendy

CONTENTS

9	Some Devil's Dirty Laundry
11	One Dead Tree
13	Two Kites
17	Even Though I'm Hiding
27	Ragged White Ice
33	Flashlights in the Snow
35	For Scotland
39	River Water
45	Black Arts
47	Great Ceremony
51	Birds in the Bush
55	Red Push-Pins
57	Old Iron
63	Oh Jesus
69	Picasso's in Prison
75	Fern Leaves Unfurling in the Dark Green Shade
81	My Kick in the Nuts from Karma
87	The Squirrel That Sees That a Dog in the Park Sees It
91	Cookie Tin
99	Little Red Speedo
111	Tentative Brushstrokes
117	Punched His Dead Face
119	Acknowledgements

SOME DEVIL'S DIRTY LAUNDRY

Smoky clouds are stretched as thin as Saran Wrap over a tired November moon. White Birch takes his calm sweet time, big boots sloshing and crunching over the just frozen field towards the welcoming, warm yellow lights of the wood frame house. It's a calm and quiet evening. No north wind scraping the dry and empty branches together. No distant dogs barking or howling at who knows what. There was only the sound of his steady footsteps that seemed to thunder down, as if he were King Konging his way along to a terrible task.

White Birch decided, without further hesitation or trepidation, that he would kill Richmond there that night.

His path was as straight as an arrow, but his mind was floating around like a dandelion spore in a baby's breath of a breeze. He thought about how wrens will teach a secret song to their newborn nestlings. When mommy bird has flown off to find a beak full of bugs to bring back to her hungry chirping young, another sort of feathered friend will visit the wren's nest, and leave her babies there as if it's an ornithological daycare centre. Fluttering back home, mommy wren sings the *passe-partout* song that the little ones have learned and must now repeat.

Chirp the wrong tune and you're up a tree without a worm.

And, as he so very often did, he wondered about his sister. Wondering again if she really had to be sacrificed for the good of himself and his brother. I don't mean sacrificed like some virgin on the great grey stone altar with Satan leering and rubbing his sticky hands together in crude anticipation. His mother was doing her damnedest, broke and on her own with three kids in the Fifties. Sister Wendy was never not in trouble. Ruined by the tender cruel tragedy of a child's innocence suffocated. Help didn't help. She went her own way. She went the wrong way.

Looking down upon his mother there in the Elders' Home, seeing her lost and confused on her death bed at 88, he felt a kind of horror that aged him, scared and saddened him. She rocked a doll in her arms, and over and over said, "I lost my baby." He knew she meant his sister Wendy.

In the stark stink of glue, shit and bad booze, he would curl up, somehow happy most nights as a boy with the warmth and love of his older brother. They took turns reading books aloud. The stories made him strong. He knew then that he could be a hero. That he *would* be a hero. He could slay all those swirling black ghosts. And still he struggled with them.

He was just standing there in that field now as solid as cement, like some gigantic king of garden gnomes. Light was seeping over the horizon. White Birch began to make out the bats. Hundreds and hundreds of bats, strung out upside down, sleeping side by side, all along the thin branches of the spare trees. Some devil's dirty laundry.

Richmond, seeing that no one was there, turned away from the kitchen window closing the blind behind him. Slowly, other lights went out throughout the house, like big cats closing their amber eyes to nap. Tattered curtains of thin clouds parted away from the dim spotlight of a now low moon. White Birch turned in his frozen tracks towards home.

ONE DEAD TREE

There is a small bar in Montreal known as "The Crossroads." This place is not situated at an intersection of two roads, as all bars, pubs or inns in this world named "The Crossroads" are meant to be. Instead, this establishment straddles the line between two neighbourhoods. Both of these areas are predominantly anglophone. Extravagantly posh and wealthy Westmount grinds up against the grittier and largely lower-middle-class district of Notre-Dame-De-Grace (NDG). Those that gym, jog, brunch and shop are sharing the same sidewalk with struggling artists, coke heads, students, tradesmen, welfare recipients and single moms.

If you sat out front on the patio cradling a beer and smoking a cigarette on this pretty spring afternoon, with newborn birds twittering, sun shining and people smiling as they pass, you could look all up and down Sherbrooke Street West at the neat rows of trees shimmering with an energetic and effervescent green, the colour of KFC coleslaw. You might see only the one dead tree. It is directly in front of you and "The Roads." This should be no surprise or considered coincidence as it is a blatant, perfect metaphor. The barren dry skeleton looms above like some dark omen of what lies within. A crazed sculptor's totem of dark warning, assembled with branches of brittle grey bones, dug up by scrawny dogs from the ashen earth of cigarette butts, dried blood and broken glass.

At the epicentre of this chaotic universe there is a pool table. Every day and every night, ragged sex, hard drugs and fierce inexorable violence ceaselessly satellite. Planets collide. Galaxies are sucked into a black hole and lost forever. Some stars twinkle, and others streak screaming across the dark lonesome sky. Like dollar store candles, most simply flicker with hope, before they quickly fade away and are forgotten.

TWO KITES

Muttering and whispering her own bad poetry she'd slink secretly along, through the cold frozen night of Westmount, the few blocks from the bar to my place. Weaving in and out between the parked cars and ducking behind trees and utility poles like a soldier evading an enemy sniper. I'd leave before her. Everyone knew but she insisted that no one know we were meeting. Natalie wanted my drugs and booze, and I wanted her insane enthusiastic sex. Hot young coke whore meets horny older guy. Our needs were honest, delineated and always satisfied. I'd smack out a few fat lines on a mirror while she slowly struggled to undress, fighting with her bra, so stoned, mystified as if she'd never worn one of these harnesses before. I'd pour some shit red wine for us, glancing over at her now free, perfect tits. Natalie never shut up. It was as if she was a tragic medium with a direct channel to another world or a worse place than this one. Always seeming to talk to herself, but I knew she wasn't. It'd keep me away awhile. I'd let her be. Let her be where she needed to be. Her mind was maybe wavering, but her body was still gymnast-muscled and sexy. The random tattoos excited me, the fire-breathing dragon and Celtic symbols just above her wonderful ass, and the hummingbirds and honeysuckles winding down her left arm from the strong round of her shoulder.

Fiddling with her dirty brown hair, pulling it back behind her tiny almost elfin ears and off of her little girl's freckly and confused face, she always asks for more time bending over the kitchen island. I study anatomy as she snorts up my blow. We do this two to three times a month, but still every time she grinds on herself for being such a pitiful "slut coke whore." Natalie's pebble grey eyes, the colour of an empty prison cell with the lights off, suddenly brighten, glowing with her private painful universe, then suddenly flat-line waiting until the drug's magic revives her. Twitching epileptic, she pushes her breath out as hard as a Great Lake swimmer. I see the confusion there in those eyes, wanting to focus elsewhere maybe on a better life, but forced to stop and stare straight at the twisted wreck of her wretched needs, stronger than any virtue. I see myself there too, a distant shifting shadow in the audience near the back door of the "no-rules" fight reflected, floating inside her eyes tiny and searching everywhere for the exit.

Kissing her urgently I can almost smell the decay on her sweet breath. It's the sour stink of aging youth and fading beauty mingling with the rot of abandoned relationships, family and friends. Lost jobs, dead cats and aborted babies. Natalie descends, sighing softly and patiently, resigned to our little understanding, kneeling before me holding my half-limp dick between her thumb and index finger like an old cigar butt plucked out of a dirty ashtray she's about to smoke.

It was rare, but I liked it when she stayed with me for the night. Usually though, she'd just glare at me, scoop up her clothes and stomp off to the bathroom, slamming and locking the door. The water's running hard and the toilet keeps flushing. I recognize the scent of Old Spice when she emerges all shiny again. I forget and then I'm startled at how tiny she is: a hundred pounds and maybe five foot two? "Thanks," she offers quietly looking down at the floor, leaving my place and closing the door softly and almost reluctantly with a gun-metal click.

An hour later I'd find her back at the bar working some other guy. It would make me crazy angry and jealous as if she was my cheating wife. How quickly I would miss the salty taste of her and the funky animal smell that was ours. But when Natalie did stay, I'd run her a hot bath with lavender bubbles and send her in with a terry robe and a glass of wine. Proffering gifts for my wounded Goddess in the steamy mist I'd come visit her after a short while with the wine bottle and the last bag of blow. With a cold can of beer in hand I would sit myself close beside her on the toilet seat next to the tub. Natalie was so beautiful then, absurdly innocent glistening wet, babbling happy and fragile but unafraid. I'd dry her off with a big warm towel like she was a little kid and then we'd go off to my bed giggling and lay naked together in the quiet dark on our backs holding hands like stargazing lovers buzzing wide-eyed and exhausted talking about how we'd get it all back together again. Quit this shit. Two kites caught in a tree.

EVEN THOUGH I'M HIDING

Out here off of Cow Bay Road we had no car, no old horse, or even a flat-tired bicycle to ride away on. There was no kind of transport available whatsoever, except walking away on your own two feet. We did have a cat though and she was as big as most any dog I'd ever seen. She was striped, light grey on dark grey, and called Bullet.

Our father was a few years our mother's junior, another kid really and he was in the Navy. He was working as a cook down in the ship's scorching bright galley making all the meals for all the other sailors. He was stationed a hundred miles or more away from us in the city of Halifax. The ship was a big, flat aircraft carrier named "The Bonaventure," but the men called her "Bonnie" as if it was a girl. Bonnie carried over thirty tough little fighter planes and attack copters and a crew of almost two thousand men. Rarely did we see our dad. When we did, it was most often a surprise and almost always a disappointment.

My mother, like all the planet's poor and the pioneers before her, was an efficient recycler. More of a re-user really. Our school lunch was often wrapped up in empty plastic Wonder Bread bags, or artfully folded into miscellaneous magazine

17

pages. I liked that. One day it was a woman's pretty face and another time a picture of a cool car. She tried using newspaper one time but stopped that when we told her that the words were showing up on our sandwiches. They laughed at us at school, and so there were fights that we won and some that we lost. In doing our business, we may have insulted local businesses by wiping our little butts with the Yellow Pages.

Our home was a ramshackle little house, or a cottage, or maybe even a cabin on a dusty gravel road with no name. It was set well away from any town and so, making do, made sense. Our mom was mostly on her own out here with us three kids near the forest where we could smell the ocean's salt and hear the crows cawing and whales sadly moan and the boats of fishermen calling out to each other in a thick blinding fog. The rustling woods mingled with the waves of the water, both vast and shockingly beautiful and sometimes scary, all of it pushed around by the wind: a spirit we only saw when it danced with the others.

We were happy here, being nowhere. I was five. My older brother Dennis was seven and the kid sister Wendy was three or four, I guess. We were all about a year and a half apart, and so it got confusing. One day we were a year apart and then just like that, after a birthday, it was a two-year difference. Our road sloped softly to end where a shallow clear creek seemed to laugh along over granite grey stones wandering off to find the ocean. Jacques lived there by the water alone in the little log cabin that he had built. He was huge and hairy and nice. He talked French.

Our big old cat Bullet disappeared one day, which turned into three. As much as I liked Bullet, she also frightened me. She had worked on dad's navy ship for a few years catching and killing rats before she came to live with us. This was not a pretty little purring house cat that a child slept with and cuddled and petted and talked baby talk to. She was a savage beast with claws as long and sharp as a wolverine's and sometimes as dangerous as the nearby dark and creaking woods.

Bullet would often skulk off as slowly as the perfect feline hunter, slinking along like only cats do, low to the ground with unwavering and unblinking wide eyes. Sliding silently into the shadowed bush behind our house, intent upon some unseen conquest of capture, playful torture and then a slow ugly death. Bullet would return to us, jungle-strutting with a twitching and mangled prize of a chipmunk to proudly place at our feet.

After three days and nights, the bunch of us had given up any hope of our cat being alive. But Bullet did return home to us with trophies. Her face was a crazy little dartboard of pain and porcupine quills, quivering as she approached where us kids sat out back at the busted-up picnic table, taking turns carving different things like hearts and letters into the wet grey wood with a knife we found buried under a flat and rust-coloured rock. I think maybe I saw a shimmer of shame and then revenge flickering in her fierce old amber eyes like a full moon playing hide-and-seek behind fast moving clouds.

I gripped her hairy bulk in my arms tight against my chest holding her in a bear-hug as if wrestling with my brother Dennis. He and my mom took turns with the pliers yanking the needles out of the cat's face and talking to her sweet and soft. Bullet's eyes were tightened into fierce satanic slits of agony. Wendy stood back from us quietly crying. Bullet fought hard to escape the pain. She did finally struggle free leaving two screaming claw lines of blood down my arm as she leapt away. We scrambled and cornered her by a pile of muddy boots and dirty old shoes at the back door. Growling and hissing, she finally slumped down in defeat and stayed still and resigned, flattened out like some lumpy old rug across the floor, as we carefully removed the remainder of the quills. Walking away, I looked back at her, and she looked up at me defiantly. I knew she'd be gone before sunrise.

Stumbling in the half-light of early morning to the bathroom for a loud and lengthy piss, I saw that Bullet was not curled up asleep where she should be, on the mat at the door, like some mutant guard cat. My brother and I and Jacques searched the silent woods for a full day expecting to find her shredded body just past the next tree or bend in the river. We called out her name and whistled as if she was a lost dog, but we found nothing of Bullet. Two weeks went by and I missed the warm and immense weight of her on my lap that numbed my legs. Some mornings I would wake barely able to breathe with her asleep, more growling than purring upon my bony chest. I missed that too. Summers, Bullet could spend entire long lazy days asleep on the front steps like a hillbilly hound dog that we took care to step over, often twitching in her dreams or nightmares, of I wonder what.

Mom told us that Bullet was okay. She said that Bullet had probably gone off with some other cats to see what was on the other side of time. The other side of time, she said, was a big empty space where everything was a possibility. Whatever that means? She explained that Bullet was so big and tough and smart that she could handle herself anywhere she might be. Mom also said Bullet might come back home to us some day, but maybe not—probably not. My sister and I hugged as she cried. Dennis stiffened and glared down at the kitchen floor looking more angry than sad, as if Bullet had not run off, but had been stolen from us. Behind his big thick glasses that made him look both goofy and smart, he shared our mothers entrancing sky-blue eyes. Little Wendy's were very different. Hers, like our father's, were a luxurious dark chocolate brown that reflected you back at yourself like black and dangerous pools of water inviting you to dive in when you knew you shouldn't.

The intense and urgent campaign started there and then for us to have a dog. Not just a dog, but a puppy dog. Mom gave in quickly and easily, having seen our hurt at the loss of our good buddy Bullet. Our father arrived home with some sailor friends a few weeks later. When he opened the car door to step out, an anxious and very alive tiny perfect German Shepherd puppy raced straight at us drenched our faces with warm wet kisses and pulled at our shirts and pants to play. We stayed as still as cold cement waiting for our father's instructions. His orders. His three navy pals stood around us wavering and wobbling like silent drunken security guards.

"So, what do we name this stupid fuckin' dog?" our father barked, smirking and looking at his navy buddies for support. They let out some thin and empty guffaws and shuffled along the gravel, looking at each other in bug-eyed embarrassment. I yelled out "Nipper!" with conviction. "He nipped me," I said. "Yea, yea whatever, kid. Dennis, what about your big shot ideas? No? No surprise. You're supposed to be the man of the family when I'm away working, working to guard this family from Commies and creeps, shit." Dennis squirmed and stared back at him with an intense hatred. Our father wore the same big black framed glasses. He looked stupid and mean and not at all smart. "I'm not some soldier, I'm just a kid. I want to call the dog 'Scotty'—you said that you were Scottish, and so, we are too." "Scotnip" my mother announced brightly. And so it was so.

I watched big Jacques trundling steadily and carefully down the dusty road towards our place. He had his arms straight out before him like a waiter with a clumsy tray of sandwiches and sloshing fish soup. Even in this midsummer heat he was wearing his huge and ragged bearskin coat. As he drew closer to me I could see that he was sweating heavily, breathing hard, and carrying a flattened out cardboard box. When he came closer still, I saw that on that cardboard was a small flattened out animal the size of a baby raccoon. It wasn't a raccoon though. It was our puppy Scotnip. Jacques laid down the cardboard with the dog's crushed body on the steps before me. I think I saw a tear streak down his filthy face as he turned away home. He mumbled, "Je regrette mon petit homme, mais . . ." I knew what regret means.

The dog's body was like a dirty old doormat with a toy dog head stuck to it. His gleaming black eyes were wide open looking up at me and he seemed happy somehow. The big pink tongue was still shimmering wet and hung out past his perfect white teeth and gleaming black gums and the blood at his mouth. I could smell the heavy thick sting and stink of rubber and tar. His heat came up at me like a soul rising towards the empty cemetery sky scratching at my red wet eyes, making me seem to cry a little.

After Jacques helped us to bury Scotnip out back in the soft dark dirt by the rushing river, we went home, walking like little broken robots of the woods through tall dry grey grass in a numb and strangling silence. Everything thrummed, as if we'd been punched in the gut and boxed in the ears or maybe a meteorite had crashed beside us. Each of us stranded alone in our confused little kid sorrow or inexplicable shame. Back at home, there was no frantic and silly discussion or any hint of any interest from us three children in having kittens or puppies or a beast of any kind as a pet. Our enormous tiny hearts had shrunken to the size of jelly beans. We were all of us somewhat stunned and grim and silent for a few days after the disappearance of Bullet, and then this, quickly followed by the sudden death of Scotnip. A cottony foggy haze of mourning, and a slow motion of life enveloped the family. Mom looked sad, but acted all jolly, as if everything was okay and always would be. I went to the woods hoping to find new friends, an owl, a squirrel or maybe a rabbit or something.

The turtle that he brought home to us that first cool fall morning was enormous. The shell was the size of a garbage can lid. This turtle was a painted turtle. I don't mean a "painted turtle," I mean a turtle that had been painted. Someone, somewhere, at some time, with the subtle skill and sophistication of a Spanish mosaicist, had taken a considerable amount of time and effort to meticulously colour each section of this prehistoric amphibian shell. Still, it looked like a four-legged trashy Tiffany lamp escaping a yard sale.

He told us that he had carried it in his arms out of the ocean near his warship. He claimed the turtle had tried to swim away and that he had dove under the waves and caught it. He said that he punched it in the stomach a few times, proudly showing us the reddened knuckles of his right hand. "I haven't seen the stupid thing's head since," he said gruffly laughing. There was a large and rusty steel ring screwed deep into the center of the turtle's shell. Our father passed a heavy metal chain through it to secure the turtle like a vicious guard dog to the tool shed just out back.

We brought out a battered tin pail to her filled with water and a good pour of salt, just like in the ocean where she really lived. Lindy came back with a dirty cereal bowl that she snuck out of the kitchen sink. I tapped the side of the can of worms we'd been digging up and saving for fishing into the bowl. Dennis suddenly yelled, "I know, I know—wait-wait-wait!" He bolted into the house by the back door stumbling on the cinder block steps. Inside, he gently scraped and scooped up a handful of dead flies that had tried to escape through the window glass, their dried and fragile bodies piled in the sunlight along the windowsill in the living room behind the couch. The crumbly remains he scattered as carefully as stardust over the writhing worms. We looked at each other nodding in mutual self satisfaction. "Ugh," said Wendy squinching her nose.

In the morning fog, we found the giant turtle and the heavy chain gone. The pail of water and the shed were still there, lying over on their sides in the dirt and the weeds. I don't know if the turtle or the worms ate the flies but they were gone too.

Dennis and I, we were doing our best, struggling to set the shed upright again. It seemed, though, that the more we worked, the worse things got, as tools and assorted trash steadily tumbled out through the gaps between the walls and the ground. Then just like that, the shed just stood right up. It was our dad that had lifted it. Stuff was strewn across the dirt and weeds around us. We began to pick up empty paint cans, struggled and failed with the cement mixer, carried a bow-saw together, rolled a propane tank, carted rakes, dragged shovels, and sorted out no end of different smelly rags and strange tools. My shin got cut pretty bad on the saw teeth and was bleeding down into my left shoe. The blood was warm and sticky but the cut didn't hurt much. I spotted a small yellow rectangular tin with a red-tipped plastic top that I quickly picked up and handed to my brother. He held it up high above his head smiling at me devilishly. I responded with a who-cares shrug. Our father snapped it from his hand saying, "Come here you boys, I'll show a good trick. Now, stand still there by the shed and put your arms straight out with your palms up." We did as we were commanded. He filled our cupped hands with the clear stinky fluid and searched his pants pocket for his Zippo lighter and found it. I felt horror and excitement to see my hands on fire. Past the blue-orange flames and hot twisted air I saw my father's crazy-man smile. I wasn't afraid of him. I was afraid of becoming him.

It's early and the distant rustling wind is quiet. There is only the happy chatter of the sparrows talking outside on the slouching telephone wire, and a gull I can't see, faintly crying out over the ocean somewhere. In the corner of the kitchen stands a plastic bag as tall as I am, swollen with puffed rice. Without Bullet here, the mice will be in it soon. I reach in and scoop up a bowl full and carry it to the counter beside the fridge. I pour thin white and watery powdered milk over the cereal. I rescue a lone bruised banana that is under intense attack from a horde of fruit flies and slice it into my bowl as I carry it outside to the front steps to sit and eat. The grass and the gravel are still wet with the morning dew, reflecting the new rising sun a million times over in tiny mirrored droplets like a vast army of insect eyes staring back at me.

Mounted above my head, and out of my reach, is a big brass ship's bell. Our mother rings this bell to call us back home from the woods or the water. If the rings are long and slow, she is calling us for dinner. It's rare, but when the rings are short and frantic, there is trouble of some kind. Something like an accident, or a fire or another thing pretty bad. Maybe dad's home.

There is a nearby field that I like to run through that is sprinkled with purple and yellow flowers like candles on a cake. I run as fast, or maybe even faster than Superman through this magic meadow that tilts slightly upwards towards the endless clean white empty-page sky. At the very last edge of the Earth I leap into the soft strong arms of the air. Raising my hands up high, I fly through this perfect shimmering space to the forest of the great pines where I land lightly upon a strong bough, far up and out of sight of anything, or anyone. I sprawl limply aching there, dangling across the rough branches in a pitiful theatrical attempt at appearing injured. Even though I'm hiding, I want to be seen.

RAGGED WHITE ICE

Her face was grey and dry and deeply lined, reminding me of driftwood stranded on the rocky shores back home. I sat up ramrod straight on the tattered plaid couch beside my mom's sister, Aunt Anne. There was a tired and musty smell of damp ashes about her. Anne's nose was a big jellyfish blob webbed with thin red veins looking like a crumpled old treasure map where the rivers flowed blood and not water. When she spoke, it was a mumbling, sandpapery sound that I struggled to understand. Between Aunt Anne and her husband John, sat a large, alert and happy looking dog. They had named him "King." He was a caramel-coloured German Shepherd splotched with patches of black and some gold tufts over his bright and eager eyes. His long, shiny tongue dripped long lines of spit that dangled and swayed with his breathing in the hot dead air of the crowded apartment. I bent forward to see past King, to peer over at John. He noticed this, and smiled at me with his wet and baggy red eyes. He only had a few teeth left in his mouth. They were yellowish-brown and had me thinking of rotten corn. Still, I trusted his smile. He was wearing one of those white undershirts without sleeves that most men wear stained a pissy yellow under his hairy pits. The bottom half of his right pant leg below the knee was crumpled and empty, and draped off the couch like a puppet show curtain to the floor.

Across the cluttered room, my mother looked uncomfortable and embarrassed. She was lying flat out in a battered La-Z-Boy chair that was stuck on recline. My kid sister Wendy was dozing fitfully, sprawled limply across her body, sighing softly and making cute little sticky noises with her lips. Dennis stood slumping against the wall beside my mom and my sister as if he was some tough little bodyguard looking bored and pissed-off. I stared, hypnotized, at a wood-framed picture on the bumpy old wall just over his head. It was a scary painting of a long-haired skinny guy wearing only a big white diaper or maybe a dirty gym towel. He was hammered to an upright wooden cross with big nails and was bleeding a lot from his hands, feet and stomach. Some women with long, flowing white dresses and covered heads were kneeling beneath him in the blood-puddled dirt. One lady was crying, looking far up at his drooping face with tears in her eyes. A few soldiers holding spears were talking and laughing nearby. In the distance on a low hill, there were more crosses with other guys dangling off of them too. I had to wonder who they were, and what they had done so wrong.

Dennis didn't even notice the weird painting behind him. He was focused on a life-sized plastic leg propped in the far corner of the room. The leg shared the space with a no-string guitar, a crutch, and a Donald Duck umbrella. Maybe the leg was stolen, snapped off a Sears store mannequin as a prank. It just stood there propped calmly in the corner, naked except for a crumpled black sock and a scuffed-up shoe.

My father wasn't there. I didn't know why, but I did know that I didn't miss him. I did miss the trees hugging our house, and the nearby ocean always calling out to me like a friend that wanted to play.

In front of King was a TV tray crowded with mostly empty beer bottles. Abruptly, John, grunting hard, struggled to stand. Pushing himself up off the couch, he started swaying. I didn't know if it was because of the beers he'd drunk or the leg he was missing. He brushed up against the table, sending a bottle wobbling, and then hopped wildly over to the TV set. Anne reached out and steadied it, coughed, choked and then let loose a loud witches cackle. Dennis and I looked at one another with our eyebrows raised trying hard not to laugh. "Christ John! You sit back down and finish your beer before you fall down," she said. King smiled at Aunt Anne and barked brightly, his eyes sparkling with fun. John turned the big knob and clicked on the set. From the TV, there was only a bunch of static hissing noise and the screen was nothing but grey ghosts and funny flickering lines. Mumbling, he fiddled with the rabbit ears until the picture was pretty clear. It was *The Andy Griffith Show* just starting! I loved the whistling music and wished I knew how to do that. John seemed crabby suddenly. He turned and announced, "You know, sometimes I think the only way I can change my crappy life is by changing the channels on this damn stupid idiot box." I glanced over at Wendy to make sure she wasn't scared. She was fine, her big brown eyes smiling at the show and happy hugging King.

Before we took the long trip to the city, I had heard my mother in the kitchen on the telephone. She was yelling and then whispering and crying too. Mom sounded so upset and angry that I was shaking and scared. I only heard some scraps of what she was saying, "...sleazy... disgusting drunk...pervert... sweet little girl...ruined...he's sick..." The next morning, we packed all of our things into one big brown suitcase. Mom said that we were allowed clothes for three days, two books and one toy. I couldn't decide if I should bring my View-Master or Mr. Potato Head, and so I packed three books. Wendy only wanted

29

to take her rainbow striped hula hoop. My mother started to say no, and Wendy started to cry, and then Dennis said he would carry it. And that was that.

Blowing up hot dust and gravel, a big bus lurched to a stop, picking us up on Cow Bay Road to take us into Halifax. Soon, we were on a loud and shaky train to Toronto for two days and one night of green and grey and bright blue skies. Starless darkness streaking by. Our mom kept writing stuff in a notebook, and sometimes looked up. Through us, or past us. She seemed determined, not worried. Leaning against the window Dennis was reflected in the black glass. He had two heads now, with two mouths that never smiled or spoke. Wendy and I, we ran around screeching and laughing, chasing each other from car to car, up and down the length of the train, again and again and again. A navy guy growled at us to "shut up!" A bigger navy guy told him to "shut up." Grinning and nodding, he waved us over and then slowly fed us little treats of jujubes and Cracker Jacks, as if we were stray puppies or squirrels at a park. Mom smiling called us over to her.

Our mother had gone out early to get money from someone at the government so that we could have our own apartment. Dennis, Wendy, King and I were all crammed in tight together on the couch to sleep. It was lumpy and smelled of stale beer and stinky old dog farts. The air was heavy with wet heat and yesterday's cigarette smoke. Somehow, we all woke up at the very same time. Hungry, we shuffled along together into the kitchen rubbing our bleary eyes. John was there sitting on the floor, leaning against the cabinets near the sink, drinking what smelled like coffee. We stopped abruptly in a fuzzy line, bumping into each other and then silently stared. His scarred raw stump was sticking straight out of his underwear. It was like a one-eyed giant's big ugly weiner. I felt sad and strange and struggled to breathe, remembering the emptiness I felt standing still and alone at the edge of the ocean. Frozen solid in my feelings, I watched as a cold and hard wind crept steadily beneath the clouds, pushing calmly across the grey water like an evil invisible spirit leaving a plain of ragged white ice before me.

Mom came back to Aunt Anne's after a few hours. She looked really, really happy. We were all sitting together crammed on the couch with King, watching Woody Woodpecker cartoons. Together, we all looked over at her and sang out, *"Ha-ha-ha-Ha-ha-ha"* just like Woody would. She laughed and told us to hurry up and put our stuff back into the big brown suitcase. Mom said, "We're going home kids."

It was egg-frying hot again. Dennis and mom wrestled along the broken sidewalk with the heavy brown bag. I held on tight to Wendy with one hand and scraped the hula hoop along with the other. No one seemed to have anything to do or anywhere to go around here. A few people were busy with gardens in their yards, growing what looked like giant Brussels sprouts. Ugh. Mostly, though, everyone was just hanging out, drinking beer and smoking cigarettes. I don't know what they were all waiting for. We passed cars without wheels and kids without clothes. Toothless mouths spat shiny black goop. There was some pushing and shoving and some yelling. Police came. Dogs barked, women hollered and glass broke. It was dreary and grey and crowded. It was Cabbagetown. It was scary and exciting. Now it was home.

Our new place was over a fish and chip shop at Sackville Street and a busy road with clattering and clanging streetcars. Around the back alley, we climbed up steep, creaking wooden stairs that swayed some from side to side as we clambered higher. The place was huge. There was nobody or nothing in it. Our voices bounced like rubber balls, loud off the walls in the welcome silent emptiness. We loved it. Our apartment, and our lives quickly filled up with new friends and furniture and school and fun.

Our mom didn't have a job job. Because her job was to look after us, she said. She *did* work the few weeks before Christmas though, to buy Santa stuff for us. One night, she came home late and tired to her Christmas surprise. Our magic show! She sat down on the couch, still in her wet snowy coat. Standing in front of Mom, between Dennis and I, was Wendy with a shining goofy smile on her sweet little face. Sloooooowly, we raised a sheet in front of her and then we hollered out, "Shazam!" We dropped the sheet, and Wendy disappeared. After a few anxious minutes, we raised the sheet again, and then suddenly dropped it, yelling out another "Shazam!" And, there was little Wendy again, looking sly and shy, as if she had a secret she'd never share.

FLASHLIGHTS IN THE SNOW

Again, like gypsy nomads, prodded, pushed and shuffling along, we packed up what few things we had in some cardboard boxes from the grocery store and the battered brown suitcase. The Welfare people sent a truck and the big silent mover guys to fill and unload it. If Mom couldn't pay the rent or we were on the run from Dad or some debt, I didn't know. Without a goodbye to anybody, we left another neighbourhood and another school behind. I had stopped bothering to make fast friends or friends fast. The trek was never easy and always further and further into the blinding white rising sun, east along Queen Street, until we finally made it out. Out past Woodbine Avenue. This next neighbourhood was called "The Beaches."

In my new schoolyard, giant shade trees as big as everything, and brilliant green grass took the place of the grey and grim, gum-spackled and glass-trashed ancient black asphalt and heaving cement in Cabbagetown. Here, there were no parents with black eyes, red noses and slurring mouths reeking of booze stumbling up drunk to collect their ashamed and frightened children.

Here, I could run for miles on the wooden boardwalk alongside the sandy beach at the endless blue lake of an ocean.

Dogs yapped, stupidly chasing after tennis balls, or sent worried squirrels winding like electric ivy up and around all the tree trunks. Dads and kids flew crazy kites together. Dragons, eagles and butterflies. Smiling moms strolled slowly with babies sleeping pretty in shaded carriages, the wheels making the sound of trotting ponies on the planks. The peace of the woods and the laughter of the river back at home were almost all about me again. If no one was around, I might have skipped along or done a stupid cartwheel or two.

I could see the sweet triangles of sailboats, the shining crisp white cloth sliding across the water far off under the scatter of birds out there playing catch against the shimmering sky. You know, I think that maybe we were drawn here, secretly chanting to these tides. Answering to the song-spell of the searchlight moon finding us here on the ground, escaping into the dark. Looking ahead. Not up. Time was immeasurable now. I couldn't take a ruler or my clunky Timex and figure it out. I didn't *want* to stop to do the arithmetic anyway. Here, life was as big and wonderful as outer space out there. Star after shining star, streaking across a forever endless sky. It didn't matter if there was a God or not. All was us and we were It. Me, Dennis, Mom and only sometimes sweet Wendy.

Nothing ever stays still. I know that now. Even a really big rust-striped rock is riding along on our spinning planet like a kid on a Ferris wheel somewhere far away. It maybe gets nudged along in a landslide or just wears down in the hot Arabian wind or rushing cold mountain streams. But, just like everything and everyone, it never stops moving and changing. Our dreams are as real as our lives are dreams. We're just kids out after dark with our busted flashlights crashing into each other and falling down laughing, playing hide-and-seek in the velvet snow.

FOR SCOTLAND

No one knew where she was. Not the police, my mom, or the "Home." Was she kidnapped, hiding, beamed up by aliens, or did she just scream loud inside of herself and wander off? Dennis and I wanted to get on our bikes and look for Wendy. We wanted to find her and bring her home. Home to us and Mom. And we did try. We both had those cool long banana seats and high-bar Harley chopper handlebars on our bikes, which we always bombed around on, causing harmless stupid shit. We started out straight away, and a few other guys that knew us and Wendy, saw us, and joined the search party until it was suppertime.

Dennis and I, we whirled around for a few more hours, carefully checking out all the parks and back alleys, speaking to anyone we saw, asking questions about Wendy. They all shook their heads, *no*. Distraught and without answers, Dennis and I then turned southward, speeding down to and around the lakefront, our tires thrumming and slapping along the wooden boardwalk, sounding as if we had baseball cards clipped with clothespins on our bicycle spokes. No signs of her there, and so we pedalled hard back up and east along Queen Street, over to the water treatment plant. There were three big golden brick

35

buildings there. The largest, or the longest really, was set well back from the road. It looked like a prison or loony bin that I'd seen in movies. There was a huge football field-sized lawn that stretched out before it, striped with rows of flat and thick dead-green metal wheels and heavy steel doors, reminding me of submarine hatches, that were snug against the ground, hidden in the grass to trip over. People took their dogs there for a squat as they looked away, dissociating themselves from the shit and piss that someone else would soon step in.

    Dennis and I biked cautiously around behind this building where the land slanted sharply down towards the other two structures and then flattened out, before ending at an ugly long drop into the thrashing lake water below. In a dismal angry silence, we took our places at the very top of the highest rise, straddling our bicycles, looking down over the epic scene stretched out before us. The Sheriff and Deputy on our strong calm horses, gazing slit-eyed in the late day sun upon the bad guys' camp, watching as they stumbled from a smoky sleep. No, vengeful brave Indian warriors or crazed Scots, the Ladies From Hell that the Germans feared the most.

    Dennis raised an arm straight and high, making a tight vein-popping throbbing fist. He hollered, "For Scotland!" I did the same as I looked into his *oh-shit-here-we-go-again* scary ice-blue eyes. Pulling back hard on our handlebars, we popped wheelies, and then exploded down that steep hill with our front wheels as high as our heads. Our stickman legs whirling as fast as a fan on full. At super-flash speed, we flew down that slope until we sledgehammer-slammed straight into the brick wall, bouncing off into the rough scratchy grass. I lay on my back stunned, gazing at fat white clouds thinning into grey streaks, like men growing old before my very eyes. I realized I had started to laugh a little, and then to cry quietly. I was scared for our kid sister. Oh, Wendy.

I'm not certain why we did this bashing of ourselves, and our bicycles, again and again into the golden brick walls until our bicycle forks were too twisted to go again. Some force impelled us to, and so we did. Dennis rolled over towards me and flicked my nose with his thumb and finger and said, "Let's go kid." Shit, that hurt. We struggled hard to move along with our busted bikes, fighting against us up the steep hills, through the dried dog turds and thick rough grass. He took my bike finally, and hoisted it over his shoulder. I hooked a hand into his back pocket. Sad and tired, I needed him now, and he was there. I've been hitching a ride from Dennis for as long as I can remember. When finally we pushed up over the crest of the last rise, we saw a streetcar down over at the Neville Loop. We ran waving and hollering at the driver to wait, as if it was the last rescue plane out of an Arctic blizzard, and we caught it and rode her home. Each of us sat quietly in our thoughts of Wendy, both concocting stories in our heads, to somehow explain our screwed-up bikes to our mom.

RIVER WATER

The sun owned the sky that day. My mom needed to go to the hospital for some reason and had asked her friend Bob to look after me. Early that afternoon, we rode westward on the streetcar together to Broadview Avenue. There, we ran sliding down the long, steep hill behind the creepy old jail into the Don Valley far below. I wondered if maybe all those tough guys in big trouble, locked up in that grim prison, could see us outside being free and having fun. I could only faintly hear the city now. Grinding up against itself like some broken-down machine. Down here in the valley it was nice and whispering quiet, like in the library or at a summer camp in the country up north somewhere. We walked for hours without stopping or speaking under a white hot sky. This was no stroll. We marched like soldiers into battle or convicts on the run. A couple of times we saw beaver dams and huts over on the river. We never did actually see a beaver though, just the big random pyramid piles of grey sticks and branches that the river pushed hard against to get by. From school, I knew that the door to the hut was underwater somewhere, and that beavers dive down and then pop up inside to get some air, see their family and maybe have a snack.

A little later we crept up close to a noisy patch of sandy dirt where three big crows were fighting a long green and yellow garter snake in a savage scramble of dust. One crow had his claws vice-gripped across the snake's neck. Another pecked viciously at the beady eyes. The third crow flapped up higher than Bob's head, making him duck down and laugh. This kamikaze crow kept fiercely dive-bombing, ripping into the snake's thrashing body.

Walking away I felt sick enough to barf, but I didn't. The only other animal I remember seeing that day was a skinny little fox sneaking through tall and faded yellow grass the colour of his fur. We both stopped, frozen, in a sort of spell and stared unafraid into each other's clear and amber eyes for the longest time. "What is it Wayne?" Bob asked. "Nothing—it's nothing." "Come on then, let's go," he said. "Where?" I asked. "Further on."

Trudging ahead, we came upon a shady clearing that gave us a wide and open view of the Don River, moving along tired and lazy to who knew where. A giant of an old gnarly tree stood watch over the thin glistening strip. Tied high up around the thickest branch was a heavy rope, strong enough for a sailor to save his boat in a storm, with a knot near the end as big as a man's fist. Even with no wind at all, the rope swayed slightly in a small tight circle a couple of feet above the moist, dark earth. I looked up at Bob, and he looked back at me, squinting against the stabbing sunlight. He nodded slightly. Quickly, I stripped right down to my underwear. There was a bridge I could see far to the south of us, glimmering in the distance, crowded with all the cars fighting their way back and forth. They couldn't see me this far away.

I took hold of the big rope thick as my own arm, and I walked it slowly backwards away from the river as far as I could, until I stood on my toes. Taking a huge breath, I exploded into a hard fast run and just before the river's edge, planted my feet firm on both sides of the knot, swinging out high over the water, doing my best and loudest Tarzan call, "AAAAaaaaaAAAaaaaahhhHHHhh," before swinging back over the water, where I let go to cannonball-splash with a mighty ka-boom into the river.

Treading water before my next jungle-boy jump, I looked back up and over at Bob leaning against the big tree with his arms folded over his chest, smiling lightly down upon me. He looked like some handsome movie star. He seemed to be studying me fondly, like a father would a son, I suppose. I dove under the water kicking my feet hard, splashing to get all the way down near the bottom. It was murky grey and lonely there, and I didn't see anything. No fish, no old tires, no dead bodies or any beavers either. I crashed up through the surface spraying out of my pinched mouth a huge arc of water high into the air like a trained dolphin. I laughed like a goofball. "Don't drink it!" Bob yelled. We haven't had a drink of water all day, and so I pleaded, "Come on, why not?" He only said, "It's a grey river in a dirty city—can't be too good—make you sick." Turning away from him, I swallowed what water was in my mouth.

I could hear them, long before I saw them coming towards us, this gang of guys, pushing and yelling, and laughing and shoving along the dirt path. They were just having some stupid fun the way I would. Then, there they were, five guys lined up along the river bank in T-shirts and bathing suits, towels over their shoulders and holding snorkel stuff. They sneered down at me in the river as if I was a lesser being, trespassing on their sacred children's garden. The skinny pimpled kid tried to spit down on to me, but it just stuck to his face swinging from his chin, and the other boys jostled him and laughed. They hadn't even noticed Bob over in the shadows, standing against the tree trunk, until he took a step towards them into the light, and said softly, "You kids should come back another time—OK?" The boys just stared, but they seemed to sense some danger in

41

him, and so they shut up. Looking back over their shoulders, they stumbled towards the dirt path and away. The spitting kid stopped to give us the finger and yelled out, "Fuck you, freaks!" and then he ran like hell. We left for home soon after that.

On the streetcar ride east along Queen Street, I could see through the back windows the fish filet clouds spreading out low across the late day sky. I thought of having fish and chips for supper swimming in vinegar and drowning in ketchup. Bob sat silently next to me just looking out the window. He had given me his T-shirt earlier for me to dry myself, and so it was all scrunched and spotted with damp patches now. I told him he looked like a crazy-guy bum and poked him in the ribs pretty hard. He pretended to smack me in the face, hitting his open hand like a stuntman actor would. It was loud and sounded real. People in the other seats whipped their heads around at us in horror. I hung my head and hid my face pretending to be in terrible pain, my whole body quivering. We tried not to laugh. But we sure did.

I was tuckered out and bone-dry parched when I got home. Standing in front of the fridge with the door open and drinking straight from the plastic pitcher, I finished off the space-age orange Tang. With my head drooping heavily I slowly climbed the stairs to my room where I threw myself down on the bed in my dirty clothes. There was a great lot of noise later that woke me up. Sleep-fuzzy I came downstairs to see that Bob was still there. He looked like Paul Newman, sitting snug up against my mom on the couch. He also looked stupid drunk, and he was yelling along to a Johnny Cash song. He wasn't Newman of course, but Bob sure did look just like him. *Cool Hand Luke*, with his too-blue-to-be-true blue eyes was sitting right there, smashed and smirking, lounging in my living room, with his arm draped over my mother's shoulders. Bob even had his big mucky shoes up on the coffee table. I'd have been in huge trouble for that. He was hollering more than singing, "Down, down, down, that ring of fire. That ring of fire." He never once looked my way.

My mom seemed fine. She had one of those blue plastic hospital bands on her wrist and bandages wrapped all down her legs where they had taken the veins away. She looked sideways at Bob, and then over at me with smiling eyes, and silently mouthed, "Sorry honey." In the kitchen I sat alone at the table and ate fish and chips, flipping through an encyclopedia. I thought about the fox in the grass that I'd seen earlier in the day. I wondered if he drank the river water too.

BLACK ARTS

It was summer now, and we didn't have school to go to. Dennis and I stood in a loose line of guys waiting for a bus to take us up north to Bolton Camp. AKA 'Slum Kid Camp'. On the sidewalk beside us we each had a big black garbage bag bulging with our stuff. The night before, I had helped our mom iron the name tags onto all of our clothes and towels and things. It was only our last name for the both of us, because we're brothers.

Our sister Wendy wasn't going to camp. She was going somewhere else. She was going to a place to get some help with being "emotionally disturbed," mom had tried to explain. "Something horrible had happened to her that made her behave badly. It's not Wendy's fault-okay-OKAY?" She turned and walked away when she noticed me staring at the line of tears trickling onto her blouse. All I was thinking about was going to camp and maybe having fun.

I watched her cross the road with her head held way up high. I think that maybe she was a fashion model before being my mother. She had the confident elegance of a ballerina. You know what I mean. They float. Above all the crumpled candy wrappers, busted glass and cigarette butts. No hunching over like the rest of us. On the far sidewalk, she turned and waved madly, wiggling her fingers, mouthing to me, "I love you Wayne. Have fun hon!" and then, standing right up on her ballet toes with her hands cupped at her mouth, "Stick with your brother! Stay with Dennis!" I turned in an embarrassed state of shock back towards Dennis, pretending, like him, I did not know that mad woman. I knew my sweet little kid sister was sad and angry, most of the time. When she wasn't spitting and ranting, she was sitting as still as the dead: a ventriloquist's dummy crammed into its box, suffocating, staring straight back inside herself. Wendy never cried anymore. She only glared. She was a dark cloud waiting, wanting to rain. I made her a drawing covered over with black crayon. I rolled it into a tube then fastened it with a fat red rubber band. She didn't ask any questions when I asked my mom to pack it in with her stuff for the "Home." I hoped Wendy would find it right away. I hoped she would sit hunched over the drawing with her tongue sticking out only a tiny bit past her lips, the way she always did when she tried to concentrate. Madly she'd scratch away at the black waxy surface, discovering all the nice bright colours underneath, everything rainbows. She would smile and know that we loved her. That I loved her. Anyway, that's what I hoped.

GREAT CEREMONY

Fires are burning high, crackling all along the beach, fighting hard against winter's angry cold. We're those ancient Cornish Wreckers at the southernmost spike of that lobster claw of England. The hungry desperate wretches luring lost ships in a storm to our rocky shores to cruelly murder men that believe we are saviours. We drown them and plunder and burn the boats.

But no, we are just a bunch of regular guys, mostly Italians, smelt fishing off crumbling cement piers along the lakeshore. The sky is an inky octopus blue-black. Like bad memories, the chill breezes off the ice water are hurting inside. Some of the men along the shore have those growling monster machines that power big floodlights, which they calmly and carefully sweep across the lake's quiet and lonely dark water. I think of prison yards, or the coast guard searching for the dead or maybe a survivor thrashing in circles, scared of dying alone in a sad spastic spiral. I think of a speck of a spider spinning down the bathtub drain that I don't mean to kill, but do.

Wondering about Dennis, I look back at the raggedy line of friendly fires along the shoreline. I don't see my brother there anywhere. It's a painful wet cold that bites past my sweater to the bones. I'm a good swimmer and I have my Red Cross Badge now. I walk carefully though, out onto one of the piers to see the fishing action up close. The intense blinding lights burning and boring down past the rippling surface are tricks to catch the fish. They think it is the sun above them and flood in great rushing swarms to die at the feet of this god. Harsh and twinkling lures sparkling upon the water are out in front of the now faceless fishermen. And so, they are only ghostly shadows. Silhouettes. Dark shapes shifting against a darker dark sky.

I see that the nets are all homemade jobbies. I figure that they are hammered and glued and taped and strung together in shabby basements and cluttered driveways. Genius really. Contraptions, cleverly crafted from window screen, chicken wire, broken hockey sticks, tent poles, old curtain rods and whatever. Junk. Delicately, with a sweet tough-guy tenderness that a dad should show a daughter, they dip the awkward squarish nets into the lake where they slowly and soundlessly vanish like rags drowning in a sink of dirty dishes.

It's as if they count to ten in Italian, and then two or sometimes three men struggle together with the arcing pole that seems to want to snap. They lift the heavy load up out of the black wet, a loud trail of water streaming back down into the lake.

The net surfaces from the water, a writhing mass of life dying. I'm thinking one thousand fish. Small perfect silver fish the shape of arrowheads. Squirming. Flinching. Gagging. The size of my "up-yours" finger.

The fishers dump their slithering catch sliding across the pier then scrape it up with shovels into big green garbage bags and white plastic lard buckets. It's a slaughter for sure. One guy near me picks a few smelt up and gives me that I'll-show-you-boy look as he bites the heads off and swallows with idiotic drama. I meet his gaze, and give him a so-what shrug.

Out of the black dark of darkest night some other guy pushes by him almost putting him in the drink. He looks like a pudgy hairy old dwarf. "My is name Agostino," he belches. "Kid, forget that guy, that jerk! Me, I eat some of the fish myself. But, it's all for fun for me. Being out here. Understand, yes? That guy is an ass." He's speed-talking, this Agostino guy. "Oh, my poor, poor daughter Angelina. Ya know kid? What's your name anyway? What? Who? Mostly, I give all the fish to my friends. Maybe, they mostly throw it away, ha, ha," he bellows. Agostino is smiling so wide that I think his head will rip in two. The few remaining teeth are gigantic and ugly phosphorescent Chiclets in the abandoned mine shaft of his reeking mouth. With great ceremony, grave nodding, shoulder patting and hard arm squeezing, he hands me a heavy garbage bag of smelt. It's sloshing around like the inside of a giant's stomach. I smile back at Agostino. I like the old Giuseppe guy. He seems good and real. With great effort, I drag the loot with both hands, stumbling backwards off the pier and down across the pebbly beach. The electric crazy dancing fires claw madly at the night, climbing to the stars with glowing broken yellow fingers.

BIRDS IN THE BUSH

Bolton slum Camp was really pretty cool. The counsellors were decent guys, and so were almost all the other pay-as-you-may welfare kids. But, oh man, oooooh man, better than thinking or even talking about the girls at their camp across the lake, better than canoeing, archery, camping, ghost stories, dessert, arts and crafts, swimming lessons, free time, skit night, and singing sappy songs like "Kumbaya My Lord" around a campfire, Capture the Flag was definitely the most intense, and the most fun, cool, killer thing that we did at camp.

    This to me was more exciting than the multiple invitations to see an older kid suck his own dick in another cabin across the sports field. What would be the point? This weird mutant, skinny guy in a top bunk. Everyone crowded in his cabin freaked out about the freak show actually happening. He was all skeleton bones and blue-white veined naked, curled up into a tight hard ball like a Chinese contortionist. I couldn't really see anything with the shoving and laughing and yelling of crazy nonsense shit. Sucking and slurping and gagging, the guy was choking on himself over the howls of the mob chant, "Suck and blow, go go go!" As I was leaving for fresh air and sanity, the screen door thumped hard closing behind me. The noise both surprised and scared me, and I wasn't sure why.

To me, the super big thing you need to learn and remember about Capture the Flag is that it's every man for himself. Even though you're meant to be on some team. You're not. It's a game that isn't a game. It's serious shit, this. Smart is good. Fast is better. If you can't run, hide or hunt, you're gonna' be captured, crazy serious quick.

At Bolton it's done like this. There are two groups of roughly twenty campers each separated by a hundred yards of rough and complicated terrain. A muddy stream of slippery green rocks corkscrews diagonally through the middle. The playing field is also made up of grey sunburnt raw hills and then shady narrow gullies of thick brush and the darkest forest that a player needs to silently crash through. There will be cuts and scrapes. Your red blood bleeds. You will stumble over jutting roots and fall hard onto razor blade rocks. Your skin will be torn by thorns and sharp branches. To survive you must pass through here as soundlessly as snow drifting over an ocean.

Abruptly, you are alone in the silent lonely woods, sorting out how not to be captured, feeling like some scared and hungry caveman without a cave. You just can't be caught and shoved into the other team's prison. Once held there, you are a useless turd. Shamed and feeling stupid. Loser. So it's game over for you. It's out there in the dark and the flickering green of the woods that matters. You sense a presence, a tingle. You see a shadow where there was light. There is this crisp crunching sound. Friend or foe? The startled crows flap madly loud and fly up in warning. They caw and scatter, and scream like monkeys in a jungle.

The camp director, Mr. Lipidas, stands with a certain queer drama on the steps of his grand cabin, and heartily blows his silver whistle to start the game.

I'm not at all sure why, but I walked off dumbly into a clump of nearby shrubs. Entranced, I stood there, watching some fifty or so tiny grey birds jumping around in a bush, like pieces in some mystic distant chess game. The birds were as small and round and plump as my mother's meatballs. Their chirping was a bright and pretty noise. What happiness sounds like. In the grey darkness of the bush they had this damp and shabby appearance, as if long forgotten Christmas ornaments. They darted around in an urgent blur, switching places, in a seemingly random manner. Could all of this activity truly be aimless? Without purpose?

Something sharply flicked the back of my head. This pain reminded me of the only thing my brother did that I really hated. It hurt my feelings, somehow. I whipped my head around and there was Dennis. He looked as if he was sorry to bother me. "I have to take you to prison." That was all he said. Dennis did not look me in the eyes. He looked toward his camp and his flag. We walked along in an awkward silence, him following me, poking at me lightly with a stick, until we got to the crooked stream. I don't know why, but it was here that I exploded into a mad dash to try and escape. He wasn't even chasing me. I stepped onto a mossy green slimy rock and flew up into the air and then crashed hard down upon my bony little boy ass against the unkind cold rocks. I lay there in the stream with ice water pushing fast through my underwear still thinking about those scrambling little grey birds as my balls shrunk down to the size of two marbles. What nonsense or strategy was all that maneuvering about? The stilted jerky finger puppet moves they executed. There was a reason. I know that. Dennis pulled me up out of the water with those thoughts of strange little birds, with the ass of my pants all puckered, uncomfortable and embarrassed. He held me lightly by the arm and escorted me slowly and wordlessly to his enemy camp. I surrendered, doing what I could to not reveal my spongy butt. Dennis tossed me a soggy filthy towel and jogged off like some unknown Indian warrior to hunt again in the dark green forest.

RED PUSH-PINS

The deal with Mom was that we'd call her collect wherever we could or whenever we needed anything. Anything at all. She insisted that she know where we were and whether we were okay or not. Those days our home phone was mounted in a small yellowish sticky space the colour of ear wax on the kitchen wall between the sink and the fridge. Sitting down with Mom at the table a few days before we left, explaining our grand master travel plan, we unrolled a large map of Canada and handed her a little clear plastic box of red push pins.

She wept silently, her face hidden in her arms. We waited almost in a state of shame, never having hurt her before. Mom rocked and heaved a bit in her sudden grief. Sudden loss of all she lived for. Us. No one ever raised their voice or hand in anger in our home. We whispered our shared disappointment. Her beehive hairdo was looking more like an abandoned bird's nest just now and her clear and kind blue-blue eyes were a Caribbean ocean, soft tides of fear and salty tears. "Nothing I say will make you boys stay. Promise to look after each other. Wayne, don't you get your brother in trouble, understand." Together the three of us taped the big map up on the kitchen wall.

Dennis poked a push-pin right in the center of Toronto. He joked that it was exactly where our flat was on Bellhaven Avenue. Mom sort of laughed past her wet eyes and snotty sniffling nose. Dennis ran his finger theatrically along the wiggling line of the Trans-Canada Highway. "This is Highway 1, Mom." He told her how we'd head north of the Great Lakes through Sault Ste. Marie and Thunder Bay, then west through a wilderness of rushing rivers, small ancient lakes and great empty plains of wind-flattened grass, and towns with names like Moose Jaw and Medicine Hat, all the way to the high and mighty Rocky Mountains. Vancouver was on the other side, snug against the Pacific Ocean. That's where we're going, he said. So we went, and Dennis and I stayed tight until Vancouver. He found his way and I found the 'free love' and psychedelics I came for.

.

OLD IRON

Her car materialized like a mystifying miracle, or more like a deceitful mirage, grinding into the hard soft shoulder of the road, crunching crisply through the dusty grey gravel beside us. Ecstatic, I lunged at the car, wrapping my filthy fingers around the handle of the back door. Another hand slammed down hard upon the back of mine.

It had been so long we'd been thumbing without a ride that I'd maybe forgotten who's turn it was to sit up front with the driver, to entertain as our tacit payment for kindness. The line of questioning was shockingly similar from one driver to the next; "What's your name? I'm so-and-so by the way." Everyone's last name is by the way, by the way. "Where are you kids from?" Kids? Jesus. "Where are you headed? You do plan to return to school in the fall, I hope. Your parents do know where you are, don't they? Why are you going to Vancouver anyway? There are so many young people hitching west. What's out there?" Oh boy. All the Q&A and story-time chatter eventually ended in an awkward fidgety silence. Each of us left to wonder at the prospect of the other's murderous intent.

Sitting in the back though was glorious. You could relax and silently watch the green and grey scenery blur merrily by. Let your thoughts drift in the warm wind, past contented cows, yellow meadows or small pretty, winter wind-shredded towns. A time of sweet peace. You couldn't exactly smoke a joint back there behind the driver, but still maybe feel like you had.

That hand that had hammered down hard upon mine, it wasn't the hand of God guiding me. It was my brother's hand, yanking me roughly away from the car and then shoving me down into the ditch. He came jumping in right after me like some action-figure stuntman. I really thought he had come down to help me up, until he slugged me in the ear. Brenda stood looking down at our grappling, only shaking her head back and forth and rolling her eyes. After a bit of rolling around, grunting, groaning, kneeing and thumping each other, Dennis stood over me looking blasé at my bleeding nose. I looked up at him and realized that during all these years growing up together we had never fought against each other. We'd only ever fought on the same side, or alone, to protect ourselves or the others honour. I also realized it was definitely my turn to sit in the front. We laughed together when I warned him, "You're in such shit, man. I'm telling Mom."

Brushing off twigs, dried leaves, dirt, dust and blood as we came up out of that deep ditch, we were startled to see the car and driver still waiting. The rather pretty young woman behind the wheel waved a little and smiled a lot as we stomped and stumbled towards her. Dennis and I must have looked like ratty lunatics on the run, and yet she trusted us. I didn't trust that much trust, even less so when I saw that she had a cute little kid strapped contentedly into the back seat. I had to think that she was missing a wrench or two from her tool box.

Very quickly, lulled by the monotonous drone of our conversation and the rhythm of the tires pushing ever ahead, Dennis and the little kid were leaned into each other, asleep. Brenda had her head back against the headrest, her eyes were foggy moist slits. I winked at her, and she winked back at me, all sexy dreamy bad girl. What I thought of then embarrassed me, sitting right next to the pretty lady driver, her looking straight ahead at the endless charcoal asphalt, carving a perfect line through granite and evergreen. The smile on my face was as silly as a scarecrow's in a farmer's field. No wa, wa tears leaving Wawa.

◆ ◆ ◆

I was drifting off now, thinking and worrying about Wayne. I knew all that he had done this past year was acid. He said LSD stood for "Life's Secrets Discovered." What stupid shit. Half of what he saw, and most likely half of what he did, wasn't real. It was an hallucination. His existence was all twisted into crazy shapes and mysterious experiences, like those creepy-clown balloon animals squeaking inside his imagination. Both fabulous and frightening.

You had to have a strong mind of old iron to do that shit even once. I know. I'd tried it. Wayne did it every damn day for more than a year. Somehow, someway, he knew how to hang onto that handrail. I was scared for him because nothing scared him. Curiosity, not stupidity, drove him on. Without provisions or compass, he possessed an explorer's relentless mad bravery. Not vain naivety. Wayne would go anywhere, anytime, and talk to anybody about anything. Anything, but himself.

He was wide-eyed, his pupils as big and black as frying pans. He was forever sliding through the powdery snow, floating over the ice of our live's great lakes, chased by the flickering sharp dark shadows of swooping hawks into kaleidoscopic rainbow-coloured lines and throbbing patterns pulsing off of everything. Echoing infinitely. So very quietly stoned alone.

Still, he somehow managed to sit calmly and have a dinner of corned beef and cabbage or some other humble dish with his mother and brother. I was often there as well. I watched as they merrily tidied up together, laughing over the clatter of dirty dishes at the sink, then having tea with milk and sugar. Dad's cookies, ironically, dipped into their steaming mugs as they chatted gently about their day and the world. The boys teased their mother about her new Beehive hairdo, which added several inches to her five-foot-two frame. "Don't forget to Limbo when you go out the door, Mom. Limbo lower now. Limbo lower now. How low can you go?" "Ha ha, you two wise asses." In a karate master's flash, she takes Dennis by the thumbs and bends him sharply to his knees. He's laughing and howling despite his surprise and discomfort. Suddenly, shockingly they are dancing a Jitterbug around the room. Wayne and I are clapping our hands, stomping our feet, beaming with delight. Happy as he was, a sickening dark look of envy froze on Wayne's face at their spontaneous ease together. I think of a bat in the basement crawl space, screeching and unfolding its leather wings.

"Are you there Wayne? Are you with us? You seem so far away honey." "Of course, of course, yes, I am. Sorry Mom, just thinking about homework and stuff. Dinner was really great, thanks. May I be excused please? I promised Brenda I'd help her with a project. Okay?" She looks steadily without expression at his brother Dennis, but finally says, "Okay honey, but don't be late. I love you. You know that."

    Wayne sometimes tells me about the things that he saw in his perpetual state of psychedelia. He is a sort of ghost of a ghost, living inside his own skin, roaming around from room to shabby room behind the brittle parchment walls. A parasite laying eggs everywhere, eggs of himself that he will eat later from the inside out. The windows are gone now, replaced by rough angry scars of brick. He can see out through the milkiness, but no one can see him inside. He isn't hiding, he claims. He is observing, unobserved. He wants to travel across his desert of discovery alone is all. Doesn't need help or want any distractions.

"Why aren't we "us" Wayne?" "Jesus, Brenda, I can barely take care of myself most days. I don't need to struggle with your struggles too. Sorry but..." "We can help each other, Wayne." "Fuck, I've known you since I was twelve years old. What's really changed? I tell you nothing. Nothing that matters. Nothing's changed. Not just you, ok?—but no one or nobody. There's nothing to tell. So, the more people that think they know you, or about you, the more you exist—is that it? Well, tear my page out of the fucking phone book then. There's you," he says, extending his open hand at me, and I try to take it, but he draws it away, jabbing a thumb at himself, and says, "there's me. We know each other's crazy creepy shit. Isn't that enough, Brenda?" "No. No, it's not. You're not that hard-hearted. You're not so tough, Wayne. You know what I think?" He looks away out the car window, sighing, shaking his head. "I think you're crying and dying inside some solitary Spider Man superhero, or a silent brave knight, hiding within your cheapo tinfoil arts and crafts armour believing you can't get hurt." "Righhhht. A lobster dies in a pot of boiling water. Even a planet-sized granite boulder melts to lava in a volcano. We all evaporate. It's how we live. Not how we stupidly die, victims of disease, or crude and comical circumstance. The stray bullet or the lightning bolt."

I stared enraged at the back of his head for the longest time. Past him, outside the car window, I watched a pretty little perfect housewife struggling up the stairs of her perfect house with her paper bags of groceries from the car. Crazed, screaming kids circled her ankles like the enemy. Indians attacking the homesteaders. I almost went to help her. Instead, I touched Wayne's back softly, and said in almost a whisper, "You act like a three-year-old baby boy that believes, when you close your eyes, no peeking, all the bad monsters go away." Wayne slowly turned and looked back at me hard. Expressionless. I thought we'd finally talk now. When he slugged me my lower lip split wide and blood splayed onto his face and across my t-shirt and my jeans. He looked away and spat out the window. I got up close as if I wanted to kiss him. I bit deep into his cheek.

OH JESUS

Feels more like gravel being thrown down upon us from a bridge than falling rain. It's a hard cold night. We huddle together, shouldering our heavy wet packs, shivering under a skinny tree. Our spirits drown in the muddy puddles rising icy over our shoes. There is a church with flashing warm orange and amber neon lights far across the park. Thunder hammers and hollers, shaking us savage like our drunken dad crashing down in the upstairs hallway.

    These Mission places trade food and shelter for a sermon and a tepid shower. "Take me now Lord!" I shout at Dennis. He nods and laughs. We catch a glimpse of heaven and hell as the lightning shreds the gothic sky. Together, we duck and run out through the downpour and into the house of The Lord.

    "If you don't shower, you don't eat. Cleanliness is next to Godliness," the scrawny priest barks in his squeaky chihuahua voice. We strip, shuffle and then share the echoing shower room with grey and grumbling men. I imagine things, slithering pale millipedes and sticky slugs hiding happily in the dark and cozy creases of their bodies. Hunched old bony gentlemen are covered in angry sores and scratches and welts and piss-yellow bruises. A few long white hairs remain like threads scattered upon their damp skin. The poor buggers' legs bald and flaking dry from the knees down to their swollen feet, as if shaved for future swim meets. In their shaggy pubes hide, forgotten, wrinkled dicks no bigger than a light switch forever off. Their balls dangle half to their knees like two golf balls in a gym sock.

The hot shower is a glorious rebirth. A resurrection. Dennis, hands clasped over his crotch, eyebrows arched in horror, mouths *Jeeeeesus* at me from across the shower room. I wink and shrug back at him. The showers all stop at once like the disappointing end of a summer rain. An immediate awkward silence swirls ghostly around us through the steam. My mind shivers. No rainbows here. All of us shamble out, aware of some unknown danger.

A mangled midget guy in a wheelchair with half a shrivelled burnt face herds us fiercely into the dormitory. Wearing only a greyish towel that doesn't quite hide our guy stuff, we carry our drenched clothes in plastic bags. There are maybe thirty bunk beds in the dorm. The beds are occupied by grizzled men with sad and bitter eyes looking inward at all they've lost to insanity or circumstance. At the sight of us they chortle, and giggle like orphan boys, banging on the wobbly metal bed frames. We're being hazed by the good Lord's prison population. No one's pumping iron or shooting hoops around here. This is the last station where you wait for the train to the graveyard.

Wheelchair guy reappears with warm flannel pajamas for us. Sweet. He looks up at us all hard and tough, sitting silent on his tattered plaid couch cushions. Empty flaps of pant leg hang down like Barbie Doll drapes where his legs should be. He'd cripple us if he could. I glance over at Dennis and we both start to laugh like two goofy kids learning about vaginas in health class. I don't know. It's spontaneous stupid combustion.

A huge shimmering snot glob the size of a newborn jellyfish launches out my nose and arcs mathematically, beautifully up, and then down onto the bitter midget's lap. Any compassion or friendship between us immediately evaporates.

They have fed us fish-head soup. Dennis and I usually don't sleep in the dorm. All the suffocating old-fart fart smells, the horror-movie sound effects of gurgling and wheezing. My thoughts go to sticky nicotine-orange hands clutching my poor boy throat or worse. This night, though, we are totally zonked. We've hitched a long and dusty Trans-Canada Highway from Brandon Manitoba.

On the way a large, handsome and softly stuttering man gave us a lift in his forest green station wagon. There were a few random kids' toys and candy wrappers on the floor and back seat. After an hour or so, looking away as he spoke, he suggested we all share a room to save a few dollars. Dennis explained that we were God's good messengers and must press on into the unknown night to do His work. Only a few quick kilometres onward, handsome, quiet man jerked his car ruggedly over onto the highway's soft shoulder. Silently we got out of the car and stood with our packs. He leaned over towards us and rolled down the car window and stuck his large head out into the star-spattered night. Calmly he looked at each of us and then hollered "God can suck my dick!" I think I saw tears in his eyes. He tore away, pebbling us with stinging gravel. "Better God than us," I say.

In the dorm we pick our way carefully through all the bunks in the hopes of finding two that might be close together. Clean sheets and a warm blanket would be as welcome as Mom's ready breast to a cranky baby. As miraculous as the parting of the seas, we discover two unoccupied places across from each other. One is a top bunk and the other a lower. On the floor between them is what must be a Jokeland rubber vomit. The joke is, it isn't. I smell the fish soup.

65

Just when I think we're all settled in for a nice long coma before morning prayer, warm toast with strawberry jam and coffee, Dennis starts getting all frisky. He's half out of his bed whipping his plastic bag of wet clothes around likes it's a caber toss at the Scottish games and the end-game is smacking my face. I need sleep, not this. I get out of my bed and stand up and in one Ninja move grab the plastic bag and yank it hard towards me. Dennis pulls it back even harder. His bunk screeches and sways. I am so tired and so pissed off that I grab the now shredding bag with both hands and pull it back towards me with all my strength. He does not let go. His entire bunk bed with him in it falls over in slow motion. Dennis jumps down and I step aside into the fish-head slop. The fellow on the lower bunk rolls out, thudding onto the floor, continuing his stuporous sleep at this slumber party of the earth's ill-fated. Dennis actually picks the damn bag up off the floor and swings it wildly at me again, but now wheelchair guy is here. He reaches up and pulls it out of the air like he's catching a football for the thousandth time. I lunge at his wheelchair like a linebacker and slam it hard away from us and the tumbling beds. The bunk Dennis was in has begun *metal-screeeeeeching-metal* crumpling into the bunk I was in and now my bunk too, with a sickening witches cackle creak, is coming as if it were a 1990s Meccano set built by a blind, one-armed eight-year-old boy in a damp cramped basement somewhere in Saint-Louis-du-Ha!Ha! A crashing cascading domino. Ten, maybe twelve, bunks come twisting down, buckling and groaning in slow motion. For a few suspended seconds, we three freeze in the silent eye of the dormitory storm. This is like a pitiful scene after a devastating earthquake. Dennis is trying to prop up bunks. I'm searching through rubble for signs of life, or determining if someone is sleeping, passed out drunk, or cold stone dead. Wheelchair guy is yanking men from the bottom bunks and smacking them with Dennis' bag of wet stuff to try to wake them. Then, across the room he flicks a wall switch and the place is lit up like the surface of the sun. For a twitching terrifying time that stretches to the infinite end of everything, nothing moves. Silence is the only sound. Then a hell-raising, record-breaking, ghastly, baboon's-ass, murderous stinking shart is released... *brrt, braaah, THPPTPHPHHPH, phhhhhhrt, PPPPPPPPPPPPPP, pff, prtrtrtrgurtrufnasutututut, prrrt, PFFT!, PHHhhhh..., SPLPLLP, WHOooofff, poot, prrrrrvt, scraeft, ppwwarrppp, pllllllllllllllloooooaaa..., RRRRRRIIIIIIIIIIIIIIIIIIIPPPPP, fuuuuuuuurrrrrrrt, thhhppbbbb, verrrrrrrrrnnnnnttttt, hooooooonk, pbpbpbp, frr frr frrrrrampooo ag, ppppttttttttt, flurpppppppppppp...* Reminiscent of Le Pétomane but, with the rich scent of fish-head soup, subtle notes of Caribbean rum and... I do believe a hint of dog biscuit. From the wreckage of bent beds, blankets, barf and bodies, large laughter and unbroken broken men begin to stir. Wheelchair guy does a methodical headcount and is satisfied that all of his flock is miraculously safe and unscathed. He turns his now angry and narrowed eyes upon us and with unknown intent, wheels steadily at us, never lowering his chilling gaze. Most of the Mission guests lurch along behind him like a gang of hungry zombies, determined to feast upon our young flesh. Wheelchair guy is coming at us fast, but stops to fire the tattered bag of wet stuff. Dennis takes a hard shot in his jewels and buckles cross-eyed. We're backed up against a metal door to somewhere and fling ourselves through it, slamming a thick steel bolt in place on the other side. I run and Dennis limps up the stairs to the roof.

 Up on the flat gravel rooftop in our Mission-issued pyjamas, we roll and smoke cigarettes. I play my harmonica, believing I can coax a smile onto the stern face of a smudgy moon. Our clothes are scattered about us to dry. Dennis is asking me questions about Brenda again that I refuse to hear or answer. He says he'll stand guard tonight. We both sleep though. Morning light brings the screams of anxious crows. Urban roosters. Dennis, his hair as wild as a Neanderthal's, stands and throws a handful of gravel. They flap and flee, sprinkling mystical messages through the morning sky. Left with the calm cooing of invisible pigeons, we change into our now dry clothes. Warm white sun is softly pushing a heavenly mist above the wet grass below us. We have time to hurry. There is savage pounding and yelling at the door that leads to the roof. We can't fight off twenty-five guys and win. Nor can we jump down without breaking our spindly legs. We sure as hell can't go as the crow flies. Oh Jesus.

PICASSO'S IN PRISON

I had gone to visit him in prison a few years after what he had done, because I knew that no one else would and no one else knew. All bravado had been beaten and buggered out of him. Bob's face and hands were dry and creased like a crumpled-up page from the phone book. The playful bright blue eyes now a milky grey, looking inward as a guilty man should. He seemed shorter and much older, all hunched in his chair just beyond the wire mesh safety glass. "Your mother OK?" he whispered. "She is." I answered. "School?" he asked. "Doing great" I lied. "What about a girlfriend? You have one?" This was more of a demand than a question. We didn't so much talk as exchange facial expressions, slowly shaking our heads back and forth, with thin-lipped looks of regret and remorse. He told me to get a haircut.

I walk heavily out of there, hearing all the loud, lonely clanging and steel-crashing echoes, calling out behind me. Under my arm, I fumble with a large clumsy roll of ridiculous children's pencil crayon drawings, knock-offs from Picasso's Blue Period. I've promised to try and sell these drawings, and then send the money to his daughters. I get him a wall in a Toronto Beaches café gallery, where the old tie-dyed guy loves the story more than he likes the drawings. But then, lit incense falls onto the drawings, and it all burns up, and down to the ground.

From across the road we jump from the streetcar, it smells as cozy as coffee brewing on a campfire. Closer now, it typhoons around us, shards of thick choking smoke, screaming painful sirens, urgent strobing lights. Shadows and shapes, dart past muffled cries. His drawings are only raven's feathers of floating ashen black, the roaring heat sucking them up, in an angry vacuum, spitting into a starless sky. Any hope of any hope, gone.

She's wrapped snug all around me like a life jacket with her head nestled into my back, a welcome weight on the shoulders, like a kid on a piggyback ride. Brenda is sort of swaying and rocking us, like a mother would a cranky baby. I can't hear it, but I know she is crying too. I can feel the sobbing broken pulse of it rattling around inside of me.

One Sunday morning, a few years back, Brenda realizes she hasn't actually seen her mother in a few days. They've spoken on the phone some. The usual mom questions, "Did you eat breakfast? Did you do your homework?" She comes home from school after band practice and sees that most of her mom's stuff is gone. Her clothes, photographs, the watercolours of hummingbirds she'd painted long ago. Gone. A rather battered La-Z-Boy chair that her dad was always sitting in with beer in hand was upside down in the backyard. It wasn't long before he stopped coming home too. If he did show, he'd stink of it, look and sound like shit. When she tried talking to him at the kitchen table, he'd only say something like, "C'mon sweetie, please . . . just screw off." Her home wasn't one, so Brenda screwed off. The police found her shivering and asleep, sandwiched between some damp sheets of cardboard in the corner of a parking lot. Social Services, a couple of foster homes and then the girls' group home near me.

My buddies and I took over a garage in our back alley. We leaned nonchalantly against fences, feigning conversation, all the while keeping an eye peeled for an abandoned one. There was a side door densely grown over with grapey vines. We used this entrance, so we wouldn't be easily spotted coming and going. We'd hang there and shit-talk our parents, teachers or jerkoffs from school. We'd invent schemes and pranks of revenge or fun, well beyond the classic "burning bag of dog shit" gag. The Group Home girls welcomed themselves to share our secret hideaway, all boldly traipsing in one sunny Saturday afternoon, sexy and smiley, asking if it was OK. We agreed to a one-week trial. They would hang around the work bench near the small grungy window. They would smoke a lot, laugh and talk loudly at the same time, even while putting makeup on. Sometimes I'd watch the girls. The strong red ellipse drawn so carefully and perfectly around the dark wet emptiness of their mouths made me both excited and confused. A couple of times I heard my name in their conversations, but never knew what it was about.

The next weekend, Brenda and I were alone together in the garage for the first time. I was sitting on an old suitcase when she came in and nodded, hi. Brenda hauled herself up onto the scarred and paint-splattered wooden workbench against the far wall. Her denim skirt climbed quickly up her thighs. I glimpsed a white triangle in the dark up there. Brenda was older than me, probably twelve or thirteen.

Behind her was one of those cork-coloured peg-board walls, with all the shiny S-Hooks scattered about in a hundred dark holes. A big dreary Lite-Brite for dads. The tools were long gone, but you could still make out the shapes, the stencil stains of where they once were, like some gang of dusty ghosts of things undone. Promises not kept.

She pulled a pack of Players out of her bag, popped a fag in her pretty mouth, and lit it up with her big old Zippo. Brenda took a long hard haul off her cigarette, and then exhaled from between her lips while pulling a parallel stream of smoke sharply up into her nostrils, looking sophisticated and pretty cool. Her legs were crossed at the ankles swinging slow beneath the bench, swaying in and out of the dusty light. Pouty and pushing out smoke rings, she looked at me smiling with her spring green eyes and asked, "Smoke?" I stood up and shuffled over to her. She stuffed a cigarette in my mouth, pulled me close, and whispered in my ear, "You can finger me if you want, five minutes for fifty cents." Then she laughed a strange strangled laugh, pushing me away hard. This made no sense to me. All I knew about "fingering" someone I had learned from old gangster movies.

I did have some money though, somewhere in my room. Often, I'd bump into Bob late in the afternoon, out on the street somewhere. It was always an awkward surprise for me when we met like this. All boozy, he'd reach down and shake my hand, slap me on the back and give me a crumpled-up dollar bill while slurring, "Promise you won't tell your mother you saw me, OK? You promise, Wayne?" I would tell her about seeing Bob, but not about the money. I had told Brenda that I'd go and get her the fifty cents and be back. But I was scared, and I was lying. I didn't go home, and I sure didn't go and "finger" a girl in the garage.

Instead, I walked slowly along, scuffing at everything on the sidewalk. Pebbles, twigs or garbage, I kicked at it all. I wasn't too sure what to think of Bob. It only made sense that my mom would get lonely, and she needed friends too. He needed me to like him because he liked her, I guess. Bob had taught me a few card games. I learned a little about euchre, and a lot about poker. He knew some tricks too, but I had no interest. Guys that did card tricks had always annoyed me. There seemed something desperate that I couldn't trust.

He didn't live far from us. His place was just out on Woodbine Avenue, only three or four blocks away. The house was a scruffy little wooden shack. I sometimes wondered why he wouldn't paint the place. Fix it up for his family. He lived there with his wife and two girls. His wife was as pretty as my mom was. The daughters wore those frilly Barbie Doll dresses. The one girl was maybe six, and the other probably four. They were very cute and quiet. Almost too well behaved.

Guns drawn and held up high and close, the police swept silently into the place. A long stark line of light pierced past the closed curtains and shafted across the living room floor. She was found splayed, face up, on the carpeted floor. The body was lying tight up against, and with one arm under, a glass and chrome coffee table. The glass and her face were badly broken. Sparkling shards were jutting in and around her eyes and much of her neck, like satanic S&M jewellery. The children were cuddled up asleep against her. Bob was found passed out upstairs in the empty bathtub. He was snoring and stinking of booze. Bob was wearing only his boxers and holding a pencil in his right hand, resting on his crotch. There was no note. A skinny kitten stood on his wife's chest, licking the blood from her face.

FERN LEAVES UNFURLING
IN THE DARK-GREEN SHADE

Is that really my buddy Allan's mother in some shabby motel room somewhere, naked, and on her knees head resting on an ottoman, gleefully being photographed while being fucked doggy-style by a drooling Irish Wolfhound? It can't be, can it? Yet it seems it could be her. I don't know, but I do know it's somebody there being dog-fucked and merrily photographed, acting like it's an ordinary everyday hobby or pastime like macramé or jogging or frying eggs wearing pyjamas. It is somebody's mother or sister or wife or daughter and it's somebody's dog. It's weird, alarming, chilling and it's troubling. The dog doesn't care and can't. She doesn't seem to care and should. And yet they both appear to be enjoying themselves enormously. Turning a few crumply pages, I see a possibly pretty girl lying on a wooden bench in a barn with her mouth wrapped around a massive horse cock. Her mouth is forced wide open, deformed as if having some serious dental work done. She's looking straight at me all proud. We don't see the face of the horse. On the next page, she's splattered in cum. It covers her face and she's rubbing it on her huge tits. Again, she smiles at me licking her lips. Jesus. There are pictures of incestuous families all at one another, mothers and sons, fathers and daughters, grandpas and kids all doing sex things together. If these images are intended to be erotic, then why is my dick now rubbery limp and shrunken to the size of an eraser? My balls are hard and hidden far away in self-preservation and dread. I freeze shivering in the hellish heat of the high-rise furnace room. I'm sixteen and no virgin, and I trust the burning acid that rises up into my throat, to revolt against this twisted shit. I barf. I barf up my breakfast—bran flakes and bananas big time. I hear the rats rustling. Riffling through these magazines scattered across the floor like unburied dead after battle. What troubles me greatly is that this is what these people no longer want or need. This is what they throw down the chute into the garbage room where I am. What is it they covet and keep up there in those solemn locked apartments? If fifty magazines fall into the eight-by-twelve-foot cement holding cell where I labour with a heavy steel snow shovel, scraping up the trash, turning and taking seven steps to heave it up into the inferno of the furnace where an appetite for creepiness is converted and disguised as black smoke and grey ash. I sometimes find a *Readers Digest* with the address label removed as if this is a doctor's office, or a scrolled-up *Archie* comic selling sea monkeys, or an ancient issue of *Canadian Living* with recipe pages torn out, but the balance of publications are supreme smut.

This is a government-assisted low-income high-rise rental accommodation deep in the largely unpopulated hinterland of suburban Toronto. We are further financially and geographically impaired in our ability to integrate with those beyond our social strata. A prison camp for the poor. Isolated and surrounded by the barbed wire of poverty and ill health. The ruthless guards are the other inmates. The twelve-story building is architecturally austere, with its bleak palette of rusts and greys.

The lobby is a no-man's-land wasteland of litter and graffiti and fear. There are maybe eight to ten units per floor and so a hundred to a hundred and twenty apartments in total. The rent is income-based and so people are returning to the government the money given them by the government. In the parking lot there is a thirty-foot speed boat hitched to a black shiny Cadillac. To the east of the parking lot are two always busy basketball courts, and beyond that, an always abandoned kids' playground, where swings don't swing and little kids don't run and laugh or dangle with legs flailing from the monkey bars shouting, "Mom, look at me!" Mothers keep their children away from the broken glass and dirty needles.

No one knows I'm down here. That someone sees what they don't want to see again. They shuffle or stride unseen down the hall in socks or slippers, with random trash or tightly cinched little plastic bags, to the garbage room and then alone inside they pull down the heavy metal door to the chute. Alone, in secret. They feel the rising heat and smell the staggering stink but still they bend over into it, pinching their lips and nostrils looking down inside the tight square black tunnel, and listen to the sound of their garbage thumping or whisking at each floor and then fading away to a mysterious silence somewhere else. Is it all the singular detritus of one twisted guy that blows his entire welfare cheque, on this perverse obsession, pulling his dick to a rosy scabby pulp, or is it half the tenants here? I'm not certain what's worse. More is much worse. These are my neighbours from down the hall or even next door. We nod or say hello. We ride together in the elevator, commenting on the weather or with our heads bowed as if in silent prayer. Maybe it's the remarkably alert elderly woman that I see with her walker in the hallway in her quilted floral robe, thumping after her blind cat calling to it in a hissing whisper "Freedom, Freedom, come here." Maybe she is saying Freida. She explained her cat escapes from her balcony to the next apartment, where it is less than welcome, and so tossed roughly into the hall accompanied by threats of drowning, poisoning and balcony hanging. I once heard a rough Jamacian accent yell "Pudit down de trash hole anudder time Mutter!" Maybe it's him.

There is a strange stranger I sometimes see sitting on a bench at the basketball courts, watching the black kids perform their athletic magic tricks. He is tragically obese and forever sweaty. He seems to be struggling through cold porridge. His long dark hair is greasy and tied back in a ponytail. He spends hours there in his filthy XXXL Nike tracksuit, smoking cigarettes, swilling his Pepsi and crunching through a party-sized bag of Nachos. Watching what he wishes he was. Cool power and grace. They ignore him when he calls out to them, excited about a great shot or a bad foul, but are never rough or unkind. If he is sitting asleep on his bench speckled with crumbs like a sated Yogi Bear, someone will shake him gently on the shoulder to wake him as they pass. He sees them in his dreams as magnificent friends, so big and so beautiful.

There is this woman though. She is sexy in a sleazy stripper kind of way, coming and going with different guys. She has a dog she treats poorly. She pulls him along, screaming and dragging him as he tries to crap. She tried to kick him once and her high heel flew off high into the air. I laughed at a distance. She chased after it like a hobbling cripple, but the dog got to it first and brought it to her smiling. She smacked him in the mouth with it. He yelped and just lay down before her whimpering. I wanted to hurt her and take the poor dog home. She's the freak. But why do I care who it is? They can't touch me. Some images and ideas both good and bad are carved so sharply and deeply into the headstone of your memory, enduring, well past even your death. Distant voices from faraway, as faint as fern leaves unfurling in the dark-green shade, fanning out like the wings of newborn birds. Tiny tremors like earthquakes of our ghostly soul sometimes shiver through us, touching our hearts and taking our breath away. The rats scurry boldly everywhere through the garbage now, because I have been too quiet and still for too long. I stand roaring like some barbarian warrior swirling and slamming the metal shovel down hard on the cement floor. This scares them away squealing. *He's scared too.* They smell it in my sweat.

MY KICK IN THE NUTS FROM KARMA

Like the bird that mistakes the window for the sky, I hit the ground with a sudden thud, with nothing left to lose except maybe my life. I'm not too certain that I want or have the strength to tidy the mess up though. It must be so much easier to pull the pin and toss the grenade inside, close the door quietly, and slowly walk away without ever looking back over my shoulder, until I feel the rage and anger of the explosion, *kaboom and doom and gloom* and smack down to the ground, grinding gravel and glass into the heels of my hands, feeling stupid and ashamed, like I'm some kid that fell off his bike in front of his friends, and finally maybe, I get some answers on that topic of heaven and hell.

I remember the very first time I ever tried that shit. I'm in my "boss's" office after finishing a hugely successful marketing campaign for an elite theatre company. Robin's chic boutique design and marketing agency had as its clients, all levels of government and then the hot cool stuff, including book publishing, cinema, dance, theatre, music and the visual arts. We're hanging with Drabinsky, Znaimer, Pachter and Kain. Design awards, back-slapping, ball-tickling and client accolades were deliciously wafting our way. I was in my mid-twenties and touted as some graphic designer glamour guy in Toronto after a half-assed heroic romp at being a New York City art student.

Robin is delirious in our success. There is no person that "matters" in this town that he doesn't know. He commands all the connective powers of networking, like a Hindu deity's with a multitude of arms. He is a clever and talented mad genius writer of any genre or style. I am not certain of his age, as he constantly morphs between twelve years old and the Seven Sages. As pudgy as he is short, and dressed daily as a runaway private schoolboy, with his starched white shirt half hanging out, navy blue blazer, loosened striped tie askew, and crumpled grey flannel pants. A disarray of reddish-brown hair tumbles down his small brow to meet the heavily framed glasses that cover his alert and owlish eyes. He is cocky and charismatic, yet somehow lacks arrogance, forgiven by his good humour. Sniffling, he strolls and struts the twenty paces across the street from our offices to the Windsor Arms Hotel, where he is the welcome and celebrated witty king-jester of The Courtyard Café.

"Wayne, you're the best. Man, you *gotta* try this shit," he says, handing me a hundred dollar bill rolled up tightly into a tube. I am silent. My left eyebrow fully arched. He instructs me patiently, as a high school wood-shop teacher would with a powerful cutting tool, explaining it's many wonders but without any warning of the risks. How could I get hurt?

There is a cluttered glass coffee table between us. I am perched on the edge of a leather couch that is creviced, like a logger's calloused hands. Robin is sitting in his desk chair hunched over, leaning in to me. His office phone is ringing but he isn't answering. There are several perfect little envelopes no larger than my thumb strewn about on the table. There is an old-style safety razor blade taped along one edge. At the far end of the table, just in front of where Robin is sitting, there are eight regimented lines of white powder about an inch apart the length of a cigarette. "You'll like it," he says glowing. "You deserve it. You'll love it, Wayne. Sit down here," he bleats skittering in his chair sideways like a crab. "Put the end of the hundred in your nose and press a finger firm against the other nostril, and then just snort it hard and fast." He makes a loud sniffing noise and says, "No big deal right?" "I guess not."

The hole in the bedroom ceiling above me is the size and shape of the silhouette of a distant grazing cow. Day after night after day, for a few weeks, this ragged *Wylie Coyote* cartoon is what I see when I wake from, or fall into, a sweaty spastic sleep. My brother dashed into the burning building at the graveyard and found me coughing up blood and hacking on thick black smoke and carried me to safety. He has an extra room in his house, which is unfinished and unused, with a door always closed but never locked. In the room there is a bed and a bedside table with a lamp on it without a shade. I am mostly in that bed. This is my room now to get well, get "clean." He and his wife are at work each day. The children are at school. The only sounds are from outside, muffled and distant like a TV left on in another room.

I thought of Nancy lying there. How she lit the fuse. Because the sex was constant and tremendous and she was stunning and she was fun, I allowed us to go on together despite the emotional and intellectual vacuum. Maybe I was being lazy and irresponsible and unfair to us both. Cowards that we sometimes are, waiting to defer the conflict and hurt until that other "better" time that never arrives and so we watch the storm on the darkening horizon heading our way and go and hide inside under the bed with the other monsters.

She was twisted sick with jealousy and distrust. She wanted to be everywhere I was, demanded detailed accounts of my whereabouts and companions, as if prosecuting me for some terrible crime. I wouldn't endure her inquisitions, and thus, I was of course guilty of some sleazy infidelity. Enraged with my thin responses, she'd stomp off to the bedroom and throw herself onto the bed, sobbing. I'd go in after a few minutes. Blubbering, she'd pull me to her with an angry urgency and we'd fuck rough, as I tenderly wiped away her tears. All would be forgotten and forgiven. I'd tell her again, hard and straight, that it would be her that would cheat. I couldn't trust a person who couldn't trust me. I believed that they worried that I'd do what they do. Lie and cheat. She'd simply stare and smile wanly like a blow-up doll.

I was right alright. I had hooked her up with yet another job, with yet another friend working for the summer up north at a theatre camp for messed-up native kids. I went to visit after a couple of weeks, and read her face right away. I took us out in a canoe that was just waiting there by a pretty little lake. We sat facing each other sharing the warmth of the midday sun. Neither spoke. There was only the sound of my paddle strokes. The soft echoing clunk, clunk of wood on wood and the delicate rippling wake of the canoe skimming through the still clear water. I could see the different coloured rocks sitting on the sand at the bottom. A fish jumped like someone tossing a stone. I was Zen calm, but Nancy beaded in sweat couldn't seem to get comfortable. In the middle of the lake and Nancy began to cry, looking down at the canoe's skeleton of wooden ribs. Her eyes hidden by her falling hair. A short line of snot under her nostril reminding me of a spider's thread catching the sunlight. I stopped paddling. "It was only a couple of guys. "Tom?" "No, not Tom. The students. I only let one guy actually fuck me. I just sort of sucked the other two off. Sort of." I knew this day would come and that I had it coming for what I had done to Brenda all those years ago. This was my kick in the nuts from karma.

At the grocer I wait patiently in line for my turn as a sweet old lady, surely poet-poor, numbingly slow, counts out her change onto the counter at the cash. I can see her little scruffy dog tied-up outside in the falling snow, staring in at her through the window, looking impatient and concerned. I heard on the radio over breakfast this morning that in Madagascar they unbury their dead to celebrate their lives, dancing with the bones to the music of big brass bands. They do clean them up and put them back though. The birds fly high today, random specks of dust, jet planes inside my shuttered eyes moving in formation far above the tall buildings. It's nice. I like it.

THE SQUIRREL THAT SEES THAT A DOG IN THE PARK SEES IT

Brenda called me again last night, upset with her soon to be ex-husband. This will be her third divorce. I mostly blame myself for these failures. When Brenda came home to our apartment all those years ago, what she saw was me standing in the middle of the living room, in the middle of the day, with my pants down around my ankles, my dick deep inside another woman's mouth. Our eyes locked. Instantly, I froze, like a squirrel that sees that a dog in the park sees it. I don't move. I don't exist. I can't get hurt. My new friend, still on her knees, looked up and over at Brenda with idiotic ambivalence holding my dick in her hand like a karaoke microphone. I shoved her away and yanked up my pants. I looked over to see that Brenda's face was now like a waning candle, seeming to melt and fold in upon itself, twisting sadly in shock and hurt and horror. The little flickering flame drowned in its own small sad pool of wax. A serpent's hiss, and then the luxurious swirling lines of oily black smoke rising and falling as if Satan's poison breath.

    I followed after Brenda, at what I hoped was a safe distance as she slowly robot-walked to our bedroom. Leaning in the door frame, I could only watch, numb-speechless. She opened the window wide to the stale acrid air, the funk and hum of a sultry downtown Toronto summer. She wouldn't jump. We were on the second floor. My unfinished blow-jobber was hurrying along the sidewalk wiping her mouth on her sleeve.

The pillows bounced a couple of times on the sidewalk, then came to rest against a parked car. An old Volvo. Against the rising heat, our flimsy sheets fluttered sluggishly like flags of conquered lands crumpled and defeated over the scarred grey asphalt and cement. She struggled with the mattress. I took a step towards her to help, but was glared away. Groaning against the awkward weight, she pushed and pulled it along the wall down the short hall to the top of the steep stairs. I felt a sudden clutching sadness, seeing the abstract art of love stains about to be revealed in the shaming sun. Brenda stopped and rested her head against the mattress to catch her breath and gather strength. She put a shoulder to the heavy beast, and launched it down the stairs, out the front door onto Shuter Street. I soon followed, with an unfortunate bounce in my step springing across the mattress to the curb.

Brenda had always said she wouldn't do it, claiming that she couldn't, that she'd choke and vomit. Surely there was some cure or training available. Often, when we were fooling around making love, I'd try to sneak her head down there, gently pushing her southward. She'd wiggle aside giggling, leaving me feeling more foolish than frustrated. One Sunday afternoon, we were in the bathtub eating good cheese and drinking crap German white. She decided to try and please me this way. I sat myself on the edge of the tub as instructed. I flinched, and my back arched away from the cold white tiles towards her perfect mouth. She gagged and wretched, as if I'd tried to ram a stale baguette down her throat. I could hear her crying in the bedroom while I drained the tub. "It's okay. It doesn't matter

Brenda. Really it's okay, honest. It's not important." When I got to her, she was curled up on top of the damp covers in the fetal position, sniffling, glistening wet. Naked and shivering, frail and needy as a baby just born whose mother had died giving birth to her. I wrapped her up in a soft towel and held her head on my lap. I rocked her, lightly humming Billie Holiday's *God Bless the Child*. We found some sleep.

COOKIE TIN

Beethoven's Fifth. Her cell phone rings and, still yanking at her little skirt, she tells her driver they've finished. Picking up her faux-fur coat and bag, she gives him a dry peck on the cheek, lightly squeezes his balls, and mouths "goodbye, baby boy" and leaves. Wayne lights a joint and sighs. He feels a metallic emptiness like a single marble rolling around in a rusted old cookie tin. Sitting on the edge of his waterbed in his crappy Chinese robe, he wonders how he went so swiftly and suddenly from the hippy "free love" of the Sixties to paying for sex in his sixties. He lays back, shutting his eyes, taking a long pull off the joint, and then places it in the filthy teardrop plastic ashtray suspended above him. With his cheeks chipmunked holding in the smoke and casually moving his prick around, Wayne studies the ceiling fan. He likes the way he can see the blades spinning around and around, getting more and more faint, giving the illusion of fading and then disappearing, putting him to sleep. In a last explosive gasp, he allows the smoke and himself to escape.

A razor line of sun-bright light. A laser rips across his eyes, slicing open his dreams. He can hear a big dog howling, high-pitched hollering and wailing, like some poor woman being beaten by her drunken asshole husband. Wayne wakes up angry. He faintly considers suicide but then quickly decides to put the others out of his misery. Then he realizes it's just some wretched lonely old dog like himself. He's hard and aching to take a piss, but then the thought of what he doesn't need to do today petrifies him and entombs him in the sex-funk-stink of his dirty sheets. I really should do laundry, he thinks, as he stands abruptly and then following his erection, Wayne heads to the bathroom with new purpose.

Pulling the sheets from his bed, he thinks about her. He acknowledges she is his favourite, and he looks forward enormously to their Thursday nights. The apartment is cleaned and tidied. Her favourite Grey Goose vodka placed with care in the freezer. Limes and the best POM pomegranate juice are laid out. He arranges her favourite flowers, a bouquet of freesias, lilies, baby's breath and some delicate fern in a large milky glass vase placed on the side table near the front door. She always stops, bending to smell them, breathing in deeply and thanks him for his thoughtfulness. He beams demurely, smiling shyly and blushing, lowering his gaze. Wayne makes a great effort to concoct a special CD-shuffle love potion of mostly soul and R&B for the iPod. He chooses Barry White, Billy Withers, Boz Scaggs and Marvin Gaye, to begin with, and then of course Van Morrison's *Crazy Love*. They'll dance together, sticky with sweat and cum. Wayne always naked, she, wearing only high heels, and sometimes a silken scarf that tickles his nose. He nestles his face into her soft shoulder, lost and drunk in the scent of jasmine and baby powder. She is so much taller, and he is so much older. Wayne is fat, she is perfect. They share the same birthday, November 18. It must have some karmic significance or some magical special meaning. Wayne is 66. Exactly three times her age. She lets him do whatever he wants and never asks for extra cash. In return, he lets her go as soon as he finishes, however, or why ever, that may be. She has a chance to make more money somewhere else, with someone else. He avoids thinking of the other someone else's shaking and shivering it off. Only because he asked her, she has also told Wayne that he is her favourite too. He believes her, and he believes that she is his girlfriend, that she is away often on travel for business. He talks, explaining her absences, describing their happiness to neighbours, cashiers, bus drivers, bank tellers and anyone else he encounters, to the point of it being real to him and to them. So it is.

The sheets are in the wash. Still in his robe late afternoon, and spooning cold chunky soup out of the can, he clicks back and forth, searching intently, riding alone on the sad digital merry-go-round between Facebook and Gmail and sometimes POF and LinkedIn. Wayne is desperately looking for some attention, or a bit of recognition, and gets none. There is never a response to a FB "Friend" request unless it's a business, and he's ignored on LinkedIn, with only fourteen connections with strangers in North Africa and Dubai. Online dating for almost three years now, Wayne has not had more than a few short phone conversations. Twice he was quickly hung up on. Once, he only got to say hello, and then the woman rattled on in a high-pitched Irish or maybe a Newfie accent. He couldn't really understand. After nearly ten minutes he said goodbye. He did meet one woman for a drink downtown about a year ago. That she had wanted to meet in a hotel lobby bar gave him great hope and expectations. He liked her right away. She was a very cute, trim and polite Asian lady. She left after a few minutes of stilted chat, saying she needed to add money to her parking meter. Twenty minutes later Wayne finished his drink, downed hers, paid and left. No one on the school sites seems to remember him either. Not even the teachers. When he googles himself, he seems to have never existed. Even the ancestral sites come up blank. He did buy a coffee mug anyway with what they claim is his family crest on it. The design shows two rearing red lions, a sword crossed with an axe, a scrawny mermaid and an unknown yellow flower. This leaves him worried, wondering who he is, what he's ever accomplished. With no children, no siblings, and his parents gone to the grave, his mysterious anonymity makes him feel oddly free, and a little vengeful, but only as dangerous and mischievous as a playful Casper the Ghost, a prankster that no one ever sees, or wants to. He goes next, on to the news sites and comments on stories there. He always writes something right-wing myopic-stupid to solicit lefty rage or befriend the gun-packing crazed. It works. He can spend a few hours chuckling, creating and giddily responding to absurd comments, as if he's really involved in an important conversation. He gets responses and reactions. He feels alive.

The devil dog from hell that's making his life more hellish, burning up his bruised brain, goes off again like a useless car alarm inside his shrunken voodoo head. The noise of the dumb-fuck mutt, whining and yelping, rips into his hangover. His eyes are shrinking and swinging in his brittle skull, while his tongue swells to the size of a squirrel, filling his dry and pasty mouth with wet hair. His body aches everywhere, as if he's done something more strenuous than laundry. He's the sole survivor of a twin-engine plane crash high in the Andes. Everything explodes and burns, sending toxic black smoke and the acrid swirling stink of melting plastic into the endless unknown empty sky. Numbing cold and blinding snow. One leg badly broken. No food. No flares. It's him or the beast.

He puts his sheets in the dryer and starts a load of whites. From the heap of darks on the floor, he chooses a pair of sweatpants and his Tim Horton Leafs hockey jersey, then dresses to go out and confront the neighbour about his dog. In his pocket Wayne conceals a spray can of *Bear It*. Stopping in front of the small wood-framed mirror just before his front door, he briefly studies himself and considers shaving. And doesn't. He spits into his palms, uses that to slick back his hair, then sharply nods, and winks at his reflection, departing with some apprehension, bravely on his mission. He knocks on his neighbour's door not knowing who or what is on the other side, and grips his canister of spray for strength, like a bar fighter with his broken bottle. There is no answer. Rethinking his plan, Wayne is turning to leave when the door swings open. There is no vicious, growling, or muscled leaping and screaming, or tearing-of-his-flesh and gushing blood. There is only a man and a dog. The dog is not a Pitbull or a Rottweiler. The dog is a dusty, soft orange-grey coloured Airedale terrier, sitting peacefully and eerily smiling at him. The canine's eyes and teeth are gleaming. Wayne has no idea at all about this guy, but he strikes him as the Volvo-driving, history professor type. He is rather tall and slender, wearing a heavy knit, cream-coloured turtleneck sweater. Handsome square face, framed by an enormous, and enviable, full head of swirling salt and pepper hair, and a lumberjack, large red-and-white Hemingway beard. The guy remains mute, one hand on the door knob, bushy eyebrows raised like twin guillotines. He regards Wayne with blasé neutrality. Releasing his sweaty grip on his bear spray, Wayne extends his hand to introduce himself. The dog leaps immediately. He's knocked to the floor, slammed into the wall. The Volvo man is barking at the dog, "Cannelle, Cannelle!!!" yanking hard at his collar. Not hard enough. The dog is all over him. Wayne is petrified. But still he tries to cover his face and his neck rolling over into a ball. He finds his spray and blasts his own face. Wayne screams and passes out.

Wayne and Cannelle had met Stephanie at the dog run near Westmount Park. Stephanie does yoga twice a week, and volunteers with seniors most weekends. She never stops talking and smiling. Her husband is dead now, and her daughter is a lawyer far away on Vancouver Island. She says she is a painter. Sometimes they go for coffee together, tying the dogs up outside to a parking meter post. The dogs stand there, staring in at them like tiny frozen ponies. Together, they talk and laugh. They drink their coffee and eat their pastries. She always has a café au lait, and he drinks his double espresso long. They both have an almond croissant. Their eyebrows rising, and mouths yumming and scrumming with delight. Fine sugar powders their lips. Wayne doesn't speak too much. He allows Stephanie to do most of the talking. He responds with thin smiles and a variety of exclamations and concocted questions. She has a big old house in Westmount that she plans to sell soon, and then live at her country home near Mont Tremblant on the lake, with her dog. Her dog is a male Rhodesian Ridgeback. He's big and brawny and his name is Leonardo. DaVinci is her hero, she says. Wayne has seen her paintings and didn't like them at all. They're dreadful. Flowers in vases, horses frolicking in fields, and sunsets over oceans just doesn't get Wayne's gears going in the right direction. She asks if he has ever dreamed of living in the country. "Yes, very often," he replies with enthusiasm. When Stephanie asks if he is "handy," he says that he certainly is, even though he isn't. She sprinkles cinnamon on her coffee. He worries about his lie. His life.

A late November snow is just starting to fall. The thin and ragged flakes, an ashen white. The ghosts of fireflies shuffling across the sky, like kids square dancing shyly in a gym. Stitches and bandages crisscross over his right brow, most of his nose, and on and under his chin. Only the tips of his fingers protrude from the bandaging on his right hand and arm. He wears a patch over the left eye. He makes a good bad pirate.

Under a low cold iron sky, Wayne is slumped on a bench in the park near his apartment building. He looks to be recently mugged in his tattered and bloodied hockey jersey. Wayne knows he should go home, finish the laundry, and lay down on the couch out of the cold, but the Vicodin in his veins has him high flying, playing at shapes in the sky. That cloud is a Dragon, oh look, now it's a frog face. The snow tickling his face stops his game. Wayne stares out into the distance, and watches as a man plays with a dog. He throws a Frisbee high into the air, sending the dog after it. The Frisbee boomerangs back and then falls sharply. The dog leaps effortlessly, and then twists in the air with the gymnastic athleticism of a Chinese acrobat, catching the disc in his mouth, and trots it back to the bearded man. Wayne's dog died as a puppy when he was a boy. They said he was enough to look after. He sure did want one though, to be like the brother or friend he never had. Well holy fuckin' Jesus Christ, it's Volvo man and his killer "Cujo" dog. Wayne stands, steadies himself with the bench and then lumbers over to them. Busy with their fun, they don't notice him until he yanks the Frisbee from the guy's hand, and only manages to toss it a few feet away with his one good hand. The dog immediately returns it to Wayne, sits smartly, and drops it at his feet, smiling up eagerly. Wayne picks it up, and attempts to whip it hard at the dog's head and misses, hitting a tree behind them. Again, the dog returns it to Wayne and waits, beaming up at him. Wayne gets off a pretty good throw this time for a lefty and then watches a little concerned as the dog furiously runs it back to him. He looks over at Volvo guy and smiles weakly. "Cannelle? What does that mean? It's French. It means cinnamon. Hey, I like cinnamon. I love it on my toast. Nice dog."

LITTLE RED SPEEDO

In the laser-white bright morning at the Riu Palace Hotel in Mexico, Hannah and I skitter as quick as crabs over the burning hot sand. The scorching intensity has us levitating and foul-mouthing all "shits" and "fucks." In our agony, we're flipping the bird and shaking our fists at a distant and ambivalent exploding orb. Not soon enough, we discover a couple of filthy, once-yellow canvas lounge chairs, partially shaded by a shredded 'Dos Equis' beer umbrella. Having suffered the Malaysian firewalk for this shabby set-up, we are happily, but still grudgingly, resigned to circumstance. Patiently and strategically, we're laying out our towels, creams, books and sundry, when along comes this huge and hairy, crumpled and bloated, middle-aged Mexican fellow. He lurches and limps over to us, looking all this-is-dreadful-serious-business. Sweaty, scowling and belly-scratching, he arrives. Without pause, he barks, "*Veinticinco dólares americanos por el día Señor Mister.*" I glance towards Hannah, as she has studied Spanish in high school and indicated that she'd hoped to practice speaking it with the locals, or "the locos" as she called them, down here in Mexico. But no, her face is now more vapid than usual behind her movie star sunglasses. "Excuse me?" I say. An evil, playful look transforms his large pocked face. Smiling slyly, mockery in his bloodshot eyes, he says achingly slow, "Twenny five- 'mericano-dollars-for-de-day Meester-or-maybe-you-go-fuck your hand. HA!" He then horks, coughing up and out a slimy grey oyster snot like phlegm that sizzles, cooking beside him in the hot sand. Alarmed yet unintimidated, I press on with my case. "Please, listen, dear friend, we've scheduled ourselves for a couple of hours here *à la plage*, sun-bathing, and then are expected back at the resort for a light lunch with the manager. After which, we're signed on to what promises to be an exhilarating tour of some ancient ruins, followed by, most probably, getting somewhat ruined, ourselves, at the pool bar." I chortle, delighted with myself. My zinging wit, though, seems to have escaped this brute. He scans me up and down with uncensored loathing as I stand there in my absurd little red Speedo that Hannah brought for me as a "little surprise" and insists that I wear. It certainly is a surprise and surprisingly little. She repeatedly says, to reassure me, that I look sweetly cute and sort of sexy in it. And yet, I feel the fool, with my hairless protruding belly pushing ever forward, and my equally hairless stick-man legs marching ever onward. My dick has shrunk to the size of my thumb and my balls have deserted me, hiding with shame in the dark creases of my scrawny old ass. I feel ridiculous making an attempt at posing tough-guy, giving him the silent and steady "Do you feel lucky?" slitted Clint Eastwood eyes. But, this man, this monster with his hair so thick, tarmac black and luxurious, has more moustache hair then I have on my entire scrawny body. I'm thinking, that he's thinking, that I'm not too dangerous. "Twenny-five!" he barks in a saliva spray into my face. "But we..." "Is twenny-five dollars or fuck zee wind Meester-ha ha." Hannah is laying there, ever silent, always perfect, achingly beautiful and stone still, like some lost alabaster carving of a mythical virgin love goddess fallen from the heavens and washed up on the sandy Mayan shore.

Once again, I sure do wish that I knew karate or judo or some damn martial arts thing. I'll do that when I get back—take lessons for sure this time. Kung fu maybe. For now, though, I stand up straighter and put one hand behind my back to create some doubt, like maybe I have a secret weapon or something stashed in my butt crack. A gun or a knife or bear spray or maybe a laser gun to disintegrate the ingrate.

Looking out at the vibrant sun surfing steadily against the cyan sky with the popcorn clouds tumbling drunk above curling white-tipped waves, I remain Zen calm, taking deep, long meditative breaths. I wish only peace for us both. Perhaps his lame leg hurts horribly today, or he took too many bites of the worm last night with his amigos at the cantina. My mantra: *Be kind to all kinds.*

I follow the senor's shadowy gaze over to Hannah where she is stretched out tanning herself pretty much naked in her French micro-bikini. She's looking sexy, tight, fit and shiny. I can't see her eyes through her sunglasses and yet I know she's watching, and so I feel the need to man up. Her skin shimmers, glistening with the soft wavering light of a mirage. The oiled breasts and thighs glimmer invitingly beneath the sparkling light. "Your wife, she young and soooooooo pretty Meester" he says, nodding appreciatively and pouting his lips. "You are very rich, I think. Yes?" Sighing, I respond, "She is my friend, well daughter, sort of—not my wife."

Now, I try this fresh tactic of negotiation, slowly enunciating each syllable, "You said it's twenty-five dollars for the day, correct? So, that's kinda' one dollar an hour, si? Follow?" He tilts his massive head to one side and scratches angrily at a thick hairy ear. "Twenty-four hours—twenty-five dollars. I'll give you ten dollars for only two hours! Five dollars an hour, deal? *Com-*

prende?" I'm sure I read somewhere that Bruce Lee got into martial arts in his early fifties.

Just as I'm certain that negotiations are at a standstill, I see beyond my ugly enemy two figures approaching, ghosts, heat-warped and shape-shifting. They wear commando outfits and are laughing loudly and jostling one another about playfully like roughhousing puppies with B-movie lightning-bolt patches on the shoulders of their crisp khaki shirts. These guys are armed with little kid walkie-talkie radios and short wooden clubs with a bottle opener on the short end of the stick. I can't tell if they're sixteen or twenty-six. But I can see that they are identical twins. The Riu resort logo is stitched onto their shirts and SWAT-style ball caps. As they draw nearer, my antagonist takes one last lustful moustache-licking look up and down all of Hannah and only then, temporarily sated, he retreats, dragging his one bum leg slowly up the beach towards town, leaving a shallow ditch behind him in the sand.

These security guys are just boys. Good-looking kids that look smart in uniform. "WOW, WOW, WOW! Is she a Bunny, a Playboy Bunny Meester Sir?" Who? "Well, your daughter, lying just there, Sir." My daughter is now departed. Passed away. Dead. "Huh, what? Sorry. I guess, maybe then your crazy hot and beautiful wife?" *Ay caramba* guys, she's my friend, not my wife. Not my daughter. A sort of friend? The boys raise their eyebrows simultaneously, grinning at each other and suppressing laughter while glancing down at my sparsely clad and insignificant bump of a crotch. I do love Hannah but I do hate this damn Speedo.

Only Hannah survived the crash. Volvo or not, the others died on impact. They were hit straight on by an ambitious young police officer's cruiser, racing in pursuit of a stolen tow truck. He sustained critical injuries from the powerful force of the impact and soon died as a result. The tow truck was discovered a day later in a nearby quarry. The driver remains unknown and unapprehended. Witnesses at the crash scene reported that the car had spun around several times on the slick tarmac until it met the loose gravel shoulder, and then rolled over and over before landing upside down in a fallow farm field. Hannah's parents—wonderful friends—died, as did my sweet-pea daughter Anna and my wife Hazel.

As Roger and his wife were our very best friends, so too were the girls. We had neighbouring cottages and we'd spend almost every weekend and holiday together at the lake. Anna and Hannah were constant companions from birth. The two of them thought that it was no end of hilarious, and always worth a tittering giggle that their names were so alike. Hannah and Anna. Anna and Hannah. Hee-hee. Also, they took great delight in pretending that they were twins despite their obvious physical disparities. Hannah was taller than my slightly chubby Anna. Hannah, I'd describe Hannah as pretty and Anna, as cute. Blonde, brunette. Blue eyes, brown eyes. Certainly not twins.

I had stayed on at the cottage that tragic night to make necessary repairs to the docks and boathouse. No news of the chaos and carnage arrived until I got a call from the local police waking me early the next morning. So, whilst I was sipping Shiraz and reading McGuire's very fine and rough book, *The North Water*, before the warm hypnotic dance of the fireplace, my daughter's legs and skull were crushed, killing her directly. Only Hannah and I remained now. I do want us together. She is like family to me. My only family now. The question remained, has she living relatives? After dealing with the police, funerals, lawyers, insurance agencies, government agencies and so on, I wondered just what to do about Hannah and me.

With the assistance of an investigator, I came to know that she had only the one living relative, an Uncle Norbert, her father's estranged and, as it unfolds, somewhat strange older brother. It emerged that this Uncle Norbert made his residence in a trailer park known as Shady Acres just outside of the town of Coboconk, Ontario. I drove the two-plus hours out there with Hannah, to ask this Uncle Norbert if he wanted her to stay with him, or not. Take her in, and on, as if she were his own child and adopt her. It transpired that he was "living" with a large and loud, unkempt woman named Estelle and a small pitiful scruffy dog chained up outside in the muck without food or water. Hannah stayed back in the car as I took a slow methodical stroll around the property. The mutt whimpered and sank his muzzle into the muck as a pig might. Out at the back of the trailer, there was a saddening toppled-over swing set that had become one with the weeds. I struggled to believe that children had once laughed and played here. Stacked like firewood was a six-foot high pile of beer bottle empties circumventing the entire trailer and covered in tattered, wind-flapping plastic sheeting. At a quick glance, I estimated that there must have been five hundred or more cases of twenty-four empties. All of it Bavaria 5.5, the least expensive and most potent beer on the market. They were sitting on a fortune of conceivably $120 in returns. I imagined that it was the poor little mutt's task to guard that treasure.

Having called ahead, Norbert was expecting my visit and knew the reason for it. The fall colours there were pure poetry. Pretty gentle flakes of gold, slow-dancing like angel feathers falling softly all around me in a fresh light breeze. At the door of the trailer, I thought that I could make out suppressed quarrelling inside. I knocked sharply. In response I heard only a mechanical humming like a chanting robot breathing within; this was soon followed by mangy Chucky howling like a wolf that's lost the pack. Looking back at Hannah, still in the car, I saw that she was busy as always with her cell phone. I stood there a moment on the trailer's top step with my face a few inches from the rusted door and then called out, "Norbert, it's Robert, Robert Burford. We need to talk about Hannah!" I knocked again but hard this time, eliciting muffled voices but again no response. Just as I was turning away to leave, the door creaked slowly open like the lid of a crypt in an ancient pyramid. There stood a grizzled Norbert barefoot and wearing a filthy loosely-cinched green robe. Early retirement I'd bet. In the shadows behind him hovered what must be the monstrous and grubby giantess, Estelle. "So my brother's dead, huh? Not a nickel, not a damn dime." Estelle was nodding and snorting in the gloom behind him. "That her dere? That's her aye in da fuckin' car see. She stole all our money pumpkin pie. Little rich bitch. Listen, you want her so fuckin' bad Mr. Moron, you can have her slick dick. One thousand cash money right and away 'ya go cowboy. Do what you will with her. Ya know." He gives me a salacious knowing wink and, startled, I do wonder how he knows. "Now get your scrawny arse to the bank. I'll be here, waitin' fer 'ya Chief. "Me too," grumbles Amazon woman, swigging her beer. "Me too."

For the past several years, the girls had spent the summers with us and Roger and his wife at the cottage in the Muskokas. Life was perfect. Lovely. Idyllic. The little ladybugs flew around free and as happy as sunshine. Half naked, their skin growing darker, as their hair grew lighter, as they grew just a little taller and older. It was appalling and disquieting to me that around Hannah's eighth birthday that I began to notice and take a passing, perverse interest in the indention in her wet panties and the way her nipples had begun to push out against her camisole. Her teasing and naughty petulant looks of rebellion, real or imagined, had me shivering with I'm not sure what. The perhaps innocent sensual pout of her full lips and the inviting round of her little bum was all too much. The idea of her and us both aroused and unnerved me. This frightening pedophilistic desire, fortunately, was never transferred to my own daughter Anna. But Hannah had become, my still somewhat unwelcome, Lolita. I wanted to taste her though. Smell the delicate salt and fine fresh funk of her. Do all that lovers do, but should not do with a child. As long as I did nothing with her or to her, then this fantasy was all internalized and not, as yet, or ever would be realized. To get help, professional help, I needed to confess my twisted thoughts and feelings. I could not. I was not that strong.

I began to research pedophilia, not in the hopes of understanding my own warped needs but more with the idea of confronting my issue to end it. Psychiatric papers and academic articles were much lacking on the subject. Instead, I stumbled upon startling graphic images of men with children. Men having sex with children. Anal, oral, vaginal—all of it. Nothing hidden. The little kids appeared confused and frightened. Probably drugged. The photographs and the videos were all amateurish, jumpy and grainy. They were horrifying and riveting and realistic. I only spent a few short minutes looking at these troubling images before I became concerned that The RCMP would soon batter down my door and then batter my teeth out of my head. I was careful enough to delete my search history. I found something known as NN girls. This means "non-nude" and it is this, I suppose, that allows its open existence on the Web, despite how provocatively dressed and posed these girls are. They are all pretty or sultry and are aged six to twelve years. Mostly, they wear only tiny tops, sheer little panties, or doll-sized bikinis. They pose on their hands and knees, looking back coyly over their shoulder. Otherwise, they are lying on the floor, smiling, with their legs spread wide, or lifted up around their ears. Negligible thin strips of garment hide their privacy from the viewer. Very little is left to the imagination, and that must be the stimulus. Filling in the blank, if you will. How are the parents unaware? Or are the parents the predators? Viewing these photographs, I wanted Hannah more, yet strangely needed her less. The other alarming discovery—incest drawings, paintings, cartoons and short animations. Most were of excellent workmanship and thus convincingly realistic. I wondered were these obscene scenarios created from the imagination of the artists or with the aid of staged models? They depicted all manner of family combinations. Dads being sucked by or penetrating their daughters. Boys being blown by their mothers and cumming upon their smiling faces and full, fabulous breasts. Grandpas, aunties, brothers and sisters were at each other every which way. Only the dads with daughters held any lewd appeal for me. I did look at this a great deal and in great detail. I thought of Hannah and myself together in different intimate ways while stroking myself to a groaning orgasm. What to think of my scurrilous thoughts? I don't want what I want.

Sex with my wife Hazel had always been more awkward than erotic. Fellatio and cunnilingus were the "demon" acts of barnyard animals and diseased monkeys. Once, I had tried to be with her anally and she called me a dangerous degenerate, pig-dog rapist and punched my face. "I'm not some back-alley prostitute, Bob." The accidental pun got past her. We didn't speak for a week. We didn't "make love" for months. She was okay, and yet still uncomfortable with rear entry. It gave her great pleasure, but Hazel was always looking over her shoulder, distrusting my perceived ulterior posterior motives. Her fear somehow stoked my satisfaction.

Nine years have now passed with my Hannah without incident. Nothing more dangerous than my occasional erection at the sight of her. She calls me daddy and hugs me and sometimes I get tingly or half hard down there. Mostly I don't. I want her safe. Safe from me and all those other perverts. I worried a great deal about Hannah. She hasn't grieved. She never laughs or cries. She never speaks of us losing Anna, Hazel or her parents. Never speaks of us either. How we are together alone now. She is all stoic silence. I'm her daddy now. Who or what she is, I'm uncertain. No friends, no boyfriends. Hannah's unspoken pain and anger is a potential danger to us both. I have no underlying motive to "have" her and to hurt us in that way. We're both so very flawed and quietly content.

At the resort, we have separate rooms. She is, after all, eighteen and an adult now. Hannah and I cleverly accepted two keys each, and exchanged one with one another, so that in the event that we lost our key, the other had it.

At the disco in town, I've spent a great deal of time and money in a futile attempt at meeting a nice woman to dance with and hopefully bring back to the room. Drinking more, and buying drinks for the ladies, only got me more and more drunk and less likely to find romance. Only the garishly made-up prostitutes that smelled of other men's sweat and cheap drugstore aftershave took interest in me. They danced all sleazy-sexy, rubbing breasts and thighs against me, offering different sexual acts at different prices. I was painfully horny and I was tempted. But, as did most men, I had resolved long ago, to never pay for these divine pleasures. Or admit to it, if I had.

When I arrived back at my room in the hotel, the door was slightly ajar. I entered cautiously to find all the lights on nuclear-bomb-blast-bright and Hannah sprawled out spread-eagle, lying face down on my bed. Her skirt was jacked right up over her perfect young bubble ass. Her flip-flops had fallen onto the floor beneath her feet like a leper losing flesh. She was clothed, with the exception of her panties. These had conveniently disappeared. I was thrilled and yet puzzled. Gently checking her vitals, I determined that she was indeed alive and breathing. And so now, I finally look upon what I've wanted and denied myself for these past ten years. Wonderfully desirable and edibly sexy was my Hannah. I shook her shoulders lightly and called her name softly several times over. Nothing. A gift from the gods of supreme pleasure for my patience and stoic strength. Standing behind her staring at her most extraordinarily firm full butt and glistening vagina. My penis was as grand and solid as a railroad spike. Only I would know what I'd done. We were alone and she was unconscious. I began slowly pacing around her splayed perfection like I was a lion in the tall grey grass next to the wounded gazelle. I studied her. The lightly muscled round of the shoulders, the cute dimpled bum and the soft, fresh fallen snow of the inner thighs. The idea of masturbating on her suddenly presented itself to me enormously. I should do that. So crazy kinky. Maybe perversely satisfying. I believed that I'd enjoy seeing my cum showered nicely across her. I didn't know what to do. My cock and I were petrified, standing at the end of the bed erect together. The decision that I then made was to undress. I unfastened my belt, unzipped and let my khakis fall to the floor. At the lake, the girls were forever picking wildflowers for their mommies. I could see my wife scowling bitterly at the sight of a cold beer approaching my mouth on a warm and tranquil day. My penis was suddenly no longer up for it. Pulling off my briefs, I caught them on my big toe which threw me way off balance. I was hopping along on one foot at a dangerous angle with my now flaccid friend flailing recklessly, when I caught the other foot in that fucking little red speedo on the floor, stopped, then dropped hard, my forehead hitting the bar fridge. Just before losing consciousness, I looked up into Hannah's bewildered eyes.

TENTATIVE BRUSHSTROKES

Three days after he knew of his mother's death and thirteen days after her burial, Wayne and I took a bus out to Port Perry from Toronto to pick up the keys to his mom's apartment and to the car. I waited down on the sidewalk scuffing my boots. I caught a peek of a pretty lake past the tall shimmering elms. There was a ferry boat slowly approaching the shore of what looked like an island. The sun was low now, lighting up the side of the boat, which looked like a glimmering gold brick or a magical leaf in a backyard pool.

His Aunt Sadie was standing in the doorway with her lizardy arms crossed over beavertail boobs, holding the screen door half open with her fuzzy slippered foot. She glared smugly at Wayne with muted disgust, before reluctantly handing over the keys and address of her sister. His mother. Wayne muttered some filth about her and sex and dogs as he turned away.

The car was very, very sexy. It was a 1961, burnt-dusty rose Cadillac Seville. Like a bull near a matador, the crazy-big sharp fins at the back could easily pierce a careless man. This elegant beast—she was a lion hunting a gazelle, with a straight, sleek, long and low line kissing along close to the hot oily asphalt.

No woman alive, myself included could resist the sultry seduction of such power and sophisticated grace. At his mother's place, we were stricken by the smell of death and despair. Dr. Scholl's foot powder and the heavy scent of lavender. I thought of her washing his hair in the bubbly bathtub when he was a baby. Shampoo, the colour of honey. He said she'd take great care not to get soap in his eyes. Loneliness lived and died here. He knew he was partially to blame. Now here, picking through bones, pulling rings from the fingers, clawing gold from teeth, he shivered with the shame of his selfish neglect.

He spent time in the stifling silence, studying framed family photographs with the detachment of an anthropologist. It was both sweet and disquieting. He was once part of a family, and was loved and cherished. He was a person his mother had spoken proudly of on the steps of the church or around the euchre table with her friends. He was her son, and whatever twist the story needed, she'd present his attributes proudly. "He has the high school record now for the mile in Ontario. Did you know that? He travels a lot and he's a big reader. He's terribly sensitive. He sees things. *Feels things.* He gets in trouble because he's smart—*too* smart."

A sweet twittering of a bird caught their ear. He found the golden canary in a cage suspended by the kitchen window glowing like a light bulb in the late day sun. She seemed frightened and confused and probably hungry. He left everything that was there, except a picture of himself at possibly seven years of age, wearing a baseball glove, laughing on the lawn with his cigarette-smoking scowling father. He took the canary in the filthy wicker cage to the Cadillac, where he placed it gently on the seat between us.

Fiddling a while, he finally opened the tiny door and whispered, "You're free Tinker Bell." The little bird cocked its head and looked up at Wayne with black peppercorn eyes and twittered, swinging gaily on the perch as if freedom isn't about escaping but knowing that you could. Smiling lightly, he turned the key in the ignition. The car roared and then purred like a mountain lion in love. A light rain speckled the dusty windshield, reminding Wayne of tears messing up a pretty girl's makeup. As he pulled away, she saw in the rear-view mirror he'd left the screen door of his mother's place open. A strong wind was coming up, bringing a storm with it.

A few senseless clouds like tentative brushstrokes were scuffing up the pretty chalk-blue sky the next morning as we drove slowly into the town of Wasaga Beach. Wayne said he loathed the insistent nagging regret and inevitability of his infidelity. Did he mean monogamy is monotony?

It had been his father's car, he explained. He had sat in the back seat and endured many scrappy parental arguments as a kid. Over twenty years ago, his dad had smacked his mother yet again, and Wayne had stabbed him in the back of the neck with a sharpened pencil. His dad had shouldered the door open and staggered out of the car. His mother drove off and they never saw him again.

We were there to find his father, Wayne said. "To have a wee chit-chat is all—I need to know, you know?" I understood I suppose, running away from who I was, to be who I am, not yet being who I wanted. A human being trying to be humane was effort enough most days. But Wayne was aggressively different, chasing the storm that he was. Spinning furiously and blind in tight mad circles like the Tasmanian Devil on acid. I think that he, too, was searching for the calm and silent centre within the swirling oil drums, big-eyed cows and railroad ties.

We saw a boy of about eight, kicking along the sidewalk. Wayne pulled the car over and yanked the cage from the seat and then across my lap he dangled the birdcage out the window. "Hey kid, wanna bird? It's free." "I'm not allowed to talk to strangers." "C'maaaan, little man, it's a budgie not a parrot." The boy looked scared but took the bird and we took off down the road. "Get it?" he said, looking over at me.

It's a dusty-salmon dusk ahead of us. We struggled like tired turtles through the pitted sand towards the Great Lakes' edge. Lake Huron is so big and quietly strong here that her sing-song of lapping waves and blind hard line horizon is as of an ocean. The sun lingers a while longer as warm as a golden lamp inside of a distant tent. She haunts us with mystic majestic promises and ideas and ambition, toying and teasing us with hints of a good tomorrow.

The fire we have made has failed. We are left with drifting slow-swirling smoke, teary, scratchy eyes and the spectacle of the birds. The gulls and the swallows putting on a show of aeronautic acrobatics. Gulls are only vultures, scavengers that live off what others don't or won't eat. They are the street people of the sky. Swallows though are as agile and elegant as our Snowbirds. They are swift and skilled at being dangerously accurate as they speed crisscrossing the air within a feather of each other even as they pick invisible insects out of the charcoal sky. Swallows playing chicken.

In the morning we park across the street from his father's prim little house with all of its lush gardens. We watch like amateur private eyes as a heavy hunched old man followed by a shroud of fluttering butterflies stops and gently lays his hands on each bush and flower he passes, as a healer would a hopeful cripple. He looks up and waves weakly as we drive away in the Cadillac. "Maybe it's what he's done that matters. Not who he is."

Wayne is one of those guys that always sings along lustily with whatever's on the car radio, steering with his knees, gripping a warm beer in one hand and a reeking rum-dipped cigarillo in the other. He's loud and enthusiastic, but to my good fortune, he has a fine strong singing voice. George Jones, Jimi

Hendrix or Joni Mitchell, he works it. Wayne is a bass player without a band. He is my friend and sometimes a lover.

PUNCHED HIS DEAD FACE

There were just a few people mumbling together at the funeral. Aunt Sadie was the only person I recognized. Bitter old bitch shot me her usual evil eye. When I called Wendy to let her know that he'd died, she only said the man who stole her life was never alive. I knew Dennis wouldn't show. His hate for the man was dangerous. Wish I knew where Brenda was. Wish she was with me now and maybe more.

On top of the coffin there was a grainy, black-and-white framed picture of my father in his early twenties, cocky, in a pressed white sailor's uniform. I'm pretty sure I'd have punched his dead face if it had been an open coffin. I overheard he'd passed quietly in his sleep. A sturdy-looking woman with dark coffee-brown eyes and a dyed blonde brush-cut came over and stood close beside me. Just as I was sneaking a peek at her biker tattoos, she turned to me and asked brightly, "So, how did you know my dad?"

Acknowledgements

My heartfelt thanks to my children; Genevieve, Adam, Justin & Nicolas for allowing me to be both a father and a friend. My big brother Neil Mcncar for his input, ideas and so much more, Dr. Alexandra Jenkins for her tireless ass-kicking and tender encouragement, Deborah Chaplin, Amanda Earl, Mark McCawley, JoAnne Tatone, Michael Callaghan, Michael Bryson, Denis De Klerck, Julie Booker, Robin Day and Maggie Warda.

And thank you to the editors who first published some of these stories:
"Some Devil's Dirty Laundry" by *carte blanche*, Montreal
"One Dead Tree" by *DevilHousePress*, Ottawa
"Two Kites," previously published as "Flatline" by *Urban Graffiti*, Edmonton
"Ragged White Ice" in *The Danforth Review*, Toronto
"River Water" by *FreeFall Magazine*, Calgary
"Picasso's In Prison" in *The Dunforth Review*, Toronto
"Fern Leaves Unfurling in the Dark-Green Shade" by *EXILE Writers*, Toronto and *DevilHousePress*, Ottawa
"My Kick in the Nuts from Karma" by *DevilHousePress*, Ottawa
"Tentative Brushstrokes" in *Things That Matter Anthology*, Toronto
"Cookie Tin" by *DevilHousePress*, Ottawa

David Menear, a father of four, has spent most of his life between Toronto and Montreal, but has also lived in big city England, and quaint village France. He studied art in New York City. He began writing fiction in 2013 at the age of 59. David has won numerous international advertising awards for his creativity. His singer/songwriter work can be found on YouTube and CBC Music. Now, acting for film and television also keeps him busy. David is back in Toronto at 'The Beach', writing hard and playing tennis with terrifying enthusiasm and some certain mediocrity.

Selected Titles From Mansfield Press

POETRY

Tara Azzopardi, *Last Stop, Lonesome Town*
Nelson Ball, *In This Thin Rain*
Nelson Ball, *Some Mornings*
Nelson Ball, *Chewing Water*
Nelson Ball, *Walking*
Gary Barwin, *Moon Baboon Canoe*
Samantha Bernstein, *Spit on the Devil*
George Bowering, *Teeth: Poems 2006–2011*
Stephen Brockwell, *All of Us Reticent, Here, Together*
Stephen Brockwell, *Complete Surprising Fragments of Improbable Books*
Alice Burdick, *Book of Short Sentences*
Alice Burdick, *Flutter*
Alice Burdick, *Holler*
Sarah Burgoyne, *Saint Twin*
Jason Camlot, *What The World Said*
Laura Cok, *Doubter's Hymnal*
Pino Coluccio, *First Comes Love*
Marie-Ève Comtois, *My Planet of Kites*
Tim Conley, *Unless Acted Upon*
Dani Couture, *YAW*
Gary Michael Dault, *The Milk of Birds*
Frank Davey, *Poems Suitable to Current Material Conditions*
Adebe DeRango-Adem, *The Unmooring*
Pier Giorgio Di Cicco, *My Life Without Me*
Pier Giorgio Di Cicco, *Wishipedia*
Christopher Doda, *Aesthetics Lesson*
Christopher Doda, *Glutton for Punishment*
Glen Downie, *Monkey Soap*
Rishma Dunlop, *Lover Through Departure: New and Selected Poems*
Rishma Dunlop & Priscila Uppal, eds., *Red Silk: An Anthology of South Asian Women Poets*
Puneet Dutt, *The Better Monsters*
Laura Farina, *Some Talk of Being Human*
Paola Ferrante, *What To Wear When Surviving A Lion Attack*
Jaime Forsythe, *Sympathy Loophole*
Eva HD, *Rotten Perfect Mouth*
Eva HD, *Shiner*
Julie Hartley, *Deboning a Dragon*
James Hawes, *Breakfast with a Heron*
Jason Heroux, *Amusement Park of Constant Sorrow*
Jason Heroux, *Hard Work Cheering Up Sad Machines*
Jason Heroux, *Natural Capital*
John B. Lee, *In the Terrible Weather of Guns*
Joshua Levy, *The Loudest Thing*
D.A. Lockhart, *The Gravel Lot That Was Montana*
Jeanette Lynes, *The Aging Cheerleader's Alphabet*
David W. McFadden, *Abnormal Brain Sonnets*
David W. McFadden, *Be Calm, Honey*
David W. McFadden, *Shouting Your Name Down the Well: Tankas and Haiku*

David W. McFadden, *What's the Score?*
rob mclennan, *A halt, which is empty*
Kathryn Mockler, *The Purpose Pitch*
Nathaniel G. Moore, *Goodbye Horses*
Leigh Nash, *Goodbye, Ukulele*
Lillian Necakov, *The Bone Broker*
Lillian Necakov, *Hooligans*
Peter Norman, *At the Gates of the Theme Park*
Peter Norman, *Water Damage*
Natasha Nuhanovic, *Stray Dog Embassy*
Catherine Owen & Joe Rosenblatt, *Dog*
Corrado Paina, *Cinematic Taxi*
Nick Papaxanthos, *Love Me Tender*
Branka Petrovic, *Mechanics of a Gaze*
Shannon Quinn, *Nightlight for Children of Insomniacs*
Stuart Ross et al., *Our Days in Vaudeville*
Jim Smith, *Back Off, Assassin! New and Selected Poems*
Jim Smith, *Happy Birthday, Nicanor Parra*
Robert Earl Stewart, *Campfire Radio Rhapsody*
Meaghan Strimas, *Yes or Nope*
Meaghan Strimas & Priscila Uppal, *Another Dysfunctional Cancer Poem Anthology*
Carey Toane, *The Crystal Palace*
Aaron Tucker, *Punchlines*
Priscila Uppal, *Sabotage*
Priscila Uppal, *Summer Sport: Poems*
Priscila Uppal, *Winter Sport: Poems*
Priscila Uppal, *On Second Thought*
Steve Venright, *Floors of Enduring Beauty*
Brian Wickers, *Stations of the Lost*
Tara-Michelle Ziniuk, *Whatever, Iceberg*

FICTION

Marianne Apostolides, *The Lucky Child*
Sarah Dearing, *The Art of Sufficient Conclusions*
Salvatore Difalco, *Mean Season*
Paula Eisenstein, *Flip Turn*
Sara Heinonen, *Dear Leaves, I Miss You All*
Jason Heroux, *Amusement Park of Constant Sorrow*
Kasia Jaronczyk, *Lemons*
Christine Miscione, *Carafola*
Marko Sijan, *Mongrel*
Tom Walmsley, *Dog Eat Rat*
Corinne Wasilewski, *Live from the Underground*

NON-FICTION

George Bowering, *How I Wrote Certain of My Books*
Mark Cirilo, *Pizza Cultura*
Pier Giorgio Di Cicco, *Municipal Mind: Manifestos for the Creative City*
Amy Lavender Harris, *Imagining Toronto*
David W. McFadden, *Mother Died Last Summer*

For a complete list of Mansfield Press titles, please visit mansfieldpress.net